RUNAWAY TRAIN

EMBER BLAKE

STORY BUB

THANK YOU

Authors are a product of those who surround them, whether they admit it or not. So the list of thank-yous is long and growing.

Perpetual thanks to my readers for supporting me and having kept reading while I changed genres and even pen names. I'll be forever grateful. You bring out the best of me. Also, many thanks to Nicole Elise Bennett for editing this one — and I almost forgot, when I say author, I mean 'author-in-progress.' Always in progress, always learning, or writing would lose its magic.

WIN A PAPERBACK

If you're interested in winning a dedicated paperback copy of Runaway Train — and also my upcoming books, and behind the scenes stories — please subscribe to my newsletter below:

www.emberblake.com

FOR BRITISH READERS

I can't pretend that I'm thoroughly familiar with London or Dorchester. I'm an American, and though I've been to London, I was only interested in Oxford University, Cambridge, and the British Library, for my next novel.

Runaway Train takes place in locations I've not been to physically. It's my judgment — and I could be mistaken — that the specific feel of London and Dorchester didn't add or take from the grand theme and enjoyment of the story.

However, Runaway Train had to occur in London because of the following reasons:

1) Passengers disappeared on the train from Dorchester to London in past years, including a boy named Andrew.

2) The woman who told me about the actual events that inspired this book lives in London.

3) The family dynamics of the story fits life in London — Europe in general — more than in the United States.

Ember Blake

INTRODUCTION

While this book is a purely fictional story, it is inspired by a true-life crime going on for the past two hundred years. However, no character names, places, or dates resemble real people or real life. For this purpose, the country 'Najimbia' mentioned in the story does not exist and is used in an effort to avoid offending the people of the real countries where the story found its inspiration.

Runaway Train is a thriller written for entertainment purposes only. Please bear this in mind dear reader as this book is meant to tell the tale of a mother and her journey to find the truth about what happened to her family.

www.emberblake.com

PROLOGUE

I think I killed someone...

I watched the blood drip from my forehead and gather into a small pool on the porcelain floor by my feet. My heart thudded against my rib cage, and I struggled to catch my breath. It was hard to imagine how I ended up here, locked up in a stranger's bathroom with a gun in my hand.

I needed time to process and replay the reel of the past few days in my mind's eye, but the loud banging on the door outside interrupted me. I no longer could afford the luxury of time.

"Kate Mason, open the door," the police officer said in a demanding voice. "No need to hurt someone else."

"Where is Andrew?" I cried out in a shrill voice that sounded foreign to me, drops of blood spewing from my lips.

"We'll talk about it when you open the door!"

"I want my son back!"

The officer beckoned again, "Kate, I need you to open the door. Let me help you stop this mess before it gets out of hand."

Out of hand? I was dripping blood that I knew wasn't my own. I was wielding a gun that I didn't know how to use. I was so close to uncovering the truth prove everyone wrong, even though I hurt those I loved in the process — everything was already out of hand.

"Kate," the officer said. "I'm going to count to ten, and then I'll have to break in."

I closed the laptop I had rested on my lap, took a deep breath then closed my eyes.

What happened, Kate? What happened to the painter, the artist? What happened to the mother you once were?

My mind swirled with questions as I tried to make sense of who I once was. All I knew for sure was that I had to keep going when I asked myself the most important question of all: *was there anyone left that I could trust?*

Deep in my core, I knew I could only trust myself. I opened my eyes and gripped the gun. I had no choice.

1

My eyes were tired from scanning the travelers around me, yet my hyper-vigilance could not ignore my surroundings. I visually stalked every person in sight — the woman in the business outfit holding her suitcase. The young couple in front of me. The carpenter with his rusty tools. The three rows of middle-class, rich-wannabe students, not uttering a word while studying their phones; liking, commenting, and living with their heads inside a box. If only I could be as naïve and unaware.

There was also the tense lawyer with the glasses, tapping his foot and looking ahead as if he wanted to advance and sit in first class. The family of four kids with their rebellious son embarrassing his mum by bullying his siblings.

Then there was the silent woman in her sixties, hand on hand, no apparent purpose, quiet and content, not bothered with her surroundings; maybe this was her hangout, her solace.

I watched her for quite some time, intrigued by her persona. Sometimes she looked pleased, exuding an aura of inner acceptance and appreciation for her past life. Other times, regret dimmed that aura into thin air and showed the lines on her face. Maybe she was so lonely she needed the proximity of strangers and the feeling of belonging.

To something. To someone. Even as meaningless as strangers on a train.

Or, maybe, she was like me, desperately looking for a familiar face on this predictable train.

I've been riding this train for years. Each day booking the same route my son and husband took eight years ago. Searching, investigating, and speculating what could have happened. Each day I found myself no closer than I was the day before. Yet, I could not ignore the compelling feeling within my being that I would indeed find answers on this train.

Answers never came, not even a slither of a clue. Just people. Just life. Repetitive and monotonous as I was. Everyone hid behind the little pleasures of someone liking their posts on the phone, drinking something tasteless, or buying themselves something they could not afford.

Self-absorption and self-indulgence at its finest. All expect the gift of communication.

Everyone avoided everyone.

Seat after seat, and even shoulder to shoulder, but each inside their heads, refraining from connecting to those around them. One among the crowd, but never a crowd of one.

My fellow travelers didn't want to know about each other. They didn't greet each other, let alone a polite smile or gesture. The only way to bind this group of strangers was a tragedy.

The train conductor greeted me with a nod as he made his way to the front. He knew who I was. The sympathy in his eyes killed me every time, even though he meant well. It was just that I didn't need it. I wasn't looking for a pat on the shoulder. I knew my son and husband were dead.

It wasn't the tragedy itself that ate at my shrouded carcass of a soul. It was not knowing why or what happened exactly and the fact I never got to say goodbye.

Part of me felt they were still alive, somewhere in a far corner of the world. I knew this wasn't the case, but I could not allow myself to dispute this fantasy. It kept me going.

It gave me comfort. My disillusions were better to me than the heartbreak of unanswered questions. But today was different, it had to be. I smoothed out my skirt and exhaled.

I decided that today was my last day on the train. No more trying to solve this painful mystery. No more sympathetic looks from the conductor. No more being in the mundane. I needed to move on, to let go. I felt it was finally time.

My best friend, Emma, who was more spiritual, said it was the right thing to do so I could heal and continue my journey in life. She said letting go and living my best life was the only way to honor the departed.

I didn't blame her for her words and offerings of strength. Friends always thought that talk would help fill the silence of grief with words of hope. Had they just sat next to you in silence, they'd have done a better job.

I didn't need words to heal my wounds. I needed someone to fill the space next to me. I wished she entertained the long periods of silence I used to experience with my late husband. He knew how to say little and mean a lot. He understood the ebb and flow of my emotional needs.

Although I began to follow Emma's spiritual advice, I had never been religious. Neither was my husband, but he was spiritual. We were an unlikely pair. It was true what they say, opposites attract.

The train finally stopped at King's Cross station in London. My heart began to pound as I gathered the strength to leave it this final time. I needed to be strong. My search was over. It was time to move on.

"I'm sorry to interrupt you," his voice awoke me from my thoughts, and I tilted my head at him.

It was the voice of a handsome, tall man in a business suit. His strong accent told me he was British, not American like me. My memory of his face and particular choices of fresh, custom-tailored suits put him as someone familiar. I've seen him more than a few times on the train. I remembered him because he always seemed out of place compared to the usual crowd of exhausted travelers. In my examinations of him, I'd always wondered why he took the train when his whole demeanor oozed of money. Why take the train when he seemed to have his life planned out?

"Pardon me?" I said, half-standing and ready to leave.

I assumed he wanted my seat. He smiled cautiously, coy and sly, without saying anything further. We locked eyes, and I felt a sudden sense of calm. I froze because I couldn't take mine off his serene, blue steel eyes. This wasn't liking at first sight or even lust, but I felt him somehow.

His gaze's wholesome comfort and solidarity filled me with a sense of security, and I was at ease. I could sense his intelligence and knew his eyes took everything in, just as mine did. Few people on trains had investigating eyes like his, scanning and interpreting what was happening around them like me. The same hyper-vigilance that I sought comfort in, taking in every detail around me.

I've always been told I was an attractive woman, but I would hardly be considered it now after losing my family. I didn't put makeup on anymore, barely tried with my hair. The gym, ha, as if. Artists like me had the privilege of staying at home in their pajamas and looking terrible while painting and still making a decent living.

The eye-locking between us was on the verge of uncomfortable, and I didn't want to miss meeting Emma, so I attempted to shrug him off and leave politely. I broke his gaze and stood firmly, leaving my seat this last time. As I started to turn away from him, that's when he said it, the words that changed my life, for better and worse, "I know how you feel."

I stopped in my tracks, and my heart skipped a beat. What did he mean by that? It wasn't that I needed his sympathy or questioned why he said it. Because seriously, how dare he? My cheeks flushed with anger and embarrassment.

But something inside me decided to push the anger away. Maybe I needed someone to tell me this. To tell me that life weighed down on me and crushed my past into a thousand pieces of splintered glass I couldn't put back together.

In my confusion, I stayed frozen, not sure what to say or what was going on.

"My name is Jason Ross," he stretched out a hand. "I lost my daughter and wife on the same train."

2

EIGHT YEARS AGO...

This was the night before my life went off the rails. If I had only known the series of events that were to unfold, I would have done anything to change course.

I had made love with my husband and the love of my life, Deji Olanti, — for the last time. I should've sensed that something was off about that night. Our lovemaking was always intense and connected, but this time it felt forced and awkward.

However, his discrete crying in the shower after intimacy wasn't a good sign. I couldn't help but feel as if it was my fault, my inner voice reprimanding me to do better. Deji occasionally cried after lovemaking, and I always pretended not to know about his trauma. It was, in a sense, easier to do so than to force him to face something he wasn't ready to.

What happened to you as a child, Deji? Please tell me.

Like every other time, our lovemaking ended in his tears in the shower.

I sat on the bed, pulling my knees to my chest and fighting my own. I never understood how a powerfully built man like him dwelled in his tears after being passionate and caring for me. Early on in our relationship, there was a time when I went as far as thinking that it was me. *You're bad in bed, Kate. All your previous encounters told you that. Admit it.*

At the beginning of our romance, I'd even consulted an African American female artist I worked with. I asked her whether I needed to please him or take care of him differently as a Caucasian, pale girl from Portland, Oregon. That maybe it was a matter of interracial incompatibility. She assured me that was not the case and suggested several ways we could find pleasure and passion. I took all her knowledge to heart, and to practice, but the trials proved to be in error for Deji, and we went back to square one, no matter how the love making sessions went. I was sure it was all my fault, all my flaws, all my inexperience.

But it wasn't that. At least that's what Deji's therapist told me. Sex reminded him of his childhood. An entire lifetime of things he told his therapist but never told me. It left me feeling helpless and desperate to reach into the depths of his being.

Deji would never tell me about his childhood in Africa. Neither did his therapist. She said it was because of all the doctor's confidentiality thing. Of course, it didn't help that his therapist was also my mother, but I'll get to those complexities soon.

All I knew was that intimacy triggered memories of his suppressed past. It tore him apart from the inside out. I was left on the outside watching his inner destruction occurring time after time, unable to help. Things got worse, especially after we had our only son, Andrew.

I wish I could've been in the shower with him, wiping his tears away. Holding him together, being the glue he needed to keep from falling apart. I would often find myself with my hand on the doorknob to our bathroom, longing to be at his side, but not knowing how to do so. Instead, I was left with the pain of listening to his faint whimpering.

Did he think that I couldn't hear him? Was that why he took refuge in our bathroom, to hide his true emotion from whatever triggered his pain in the hopes that the running water of the shower would also drown out the sounds of his guttural experience?

I could hear everything. I could hear as much as his palms splotching against the walls. Frustration? Pain? It was hard to decipher. Just as hard as it was to decipher his native tongue — hearing two words over and over:

Ouna, ouna.

A Najimbian slang for *run, run.*

Najimbia was his homeland, and over the years, he taught me several phrases, taking pleasure in my accent stumbling over the words.

I wiped the tears from my face, ready for his return in my loving arms. I wasn't going to ask him questions. I wished to mend his wounds the way he had mended mine when I met him. I was only twenty years old then.

Eight years of marriage now, one would think I'd have figured it out. I never thought I'd last six months as a girlfriend with anyone — that's what my exes told me, let alone be a wife.

As I continued to wait, my mother's discerning voice taunted me in my head. Renowned psychiatrist Katherine King repeatedly advised me to leave Deji and take our only child with me.

"Men like him have been through hell in their countries, be it Somalia, Sudan, and especially Nigeria like where Deji is from," she told me last week after his session.

"Deji is from Najimbia, Katherine," I reminded her.

I'd stopped calling her mum after my dad died. I no longer felt compelled to do so as I used to call her mum only to make him happy, not her. Otherwise, I hardly identified with her as someone who loved and nurtured me — which she didn't. She was cold, frigid, never offering me the solace a daughter needed from her mother.

"They're all the same, darling," she flipped her expensive gold-coated pen between her fingers. It had her name on it and the mention of some prizes she won from the British national awards in her field. Whether she liked to admit it or not, she flaunted it about ensuring the glint of the shiny gold caught your eye.

"Third world countries traumatize their children with either war, famine, or close-minded ideologies. Yet you married into them," she cocked her head and gave me that guilt-inducing look. "I told you not to."

"I'm proud that I did, Katherine — it's not like you'd ever understand," I told her flatly. It wasn't worth my energy to get emotional.

Talking to Katherine was an evil necessity in my life. Raising my son was a financial responsibility I was not fully prepared for, and of course, we couldn't afford Deji's psychiatric therapy. So Deji and I relied on Katherine to provide him with his much-needed mental health services and a monthly stipend to bridge the gap in our finances.

It wasn't like Deji and I planned on doing it forever, but Katherine sent me a complimentary check each month for raising Andrew.

Deji objected to it, but I was the one who convinced him. Despite our strained relationship, I knew that I did not want my child to have anything less than the best. I should've trusted his judgment, but I was worried I'd raise a child into the daily struggles of the middle class where you're living paycheck to paycheck. It was also the irrational guilt of me abandoning my rich family to live on my own terms. Did I do injustice to my son by not letting him benefit from his ancestors' money?

"Oh, I understand, darling," Katherine said. "Deji is an impressive species of a man. Most African men are," she said. "I had sex with hot men when I was a young student in Cambridge. Lots of it," she leaned a little forward. "I just never married them," she said haughtily.

Over the years, I had learned to treat Katherine like a traffic jam. There was hardly anything I could do about it but wait until I reached my destination.

"I just wish I could do more for my husband," I told her. "Did he ever open up in his private session with you?"

"That's confidential, darling," she only called *me* darling if I wouldn't call her mum. "I'm the most professional psychiatrist in London. Do you think I'd make an exception and tell you? Darling?" Her words were coated with venom.

"Katherine," I grimaced. "Really?"

My gaze must have gotten to her. She fidgeted and immediately pulled out a mint cigarette from her purse, "Exposing your father was a different issue. I needed a divorce, and he wouldn't give it to me, so I dug up his sins from his past and made him suffer for it." She said nonchalantly as if it were the only choice set before her.

I shook my head. Katherine's logic wasn't logic in and of itself. It was a series of excuses where she was never wrong. But I wasn't here to talk about the past. I wanted to help my husband.

"Poor Deji," I sighed. "I wonder what they've done to him as a child."

"Ever wondered what *he* may have done to others?" She stated accusingly as she puffed her smoke upward, staring at me with glazed eyes.

"I know Deji," I said with absolute confidence through my clenched jaw as I clung to my calm composure.

"You do?"

I nodded. "It's called living with someone and getting to watch them, experiencing them, and trusting them. Truly, trust them. Then again, it's not something that you'd know about. Deji would never hurt anyone." The words came out with more malice than I intended.

Katherine took the insult like a champ. Words didn't affect her whatsoever.

"He is a Muslim African, darling," she said with a hint of judgment behind her tone, "a refugee with a scar on his right cheek. I know that must've made him look attractive at a younger age. With that body and enticing smile, looking like a buffed version of Seal, the singer from the nineties. If you trust him that much, why didn't you hire a psychiatrist from outside the family to help him?" Her condescending nature never surprised me.

"You know why," I stared at her. "The money. I couldn't afford it, let alone convince him to go to therapy. You, being a so-called family member, made him consider it. You're always nice to him but talk shit behind his back. I sometimes wonder why I'm the only one you can't do that to? Why do you have to talk shit in my face?"

"You're a version of me that I didn't ask for," she said, and it didn't hurt anymore. She said it too many times.

Having married the poor American painter in her younger years and conceived a child with him, only to grow older and realize she loved her rich family tree she descended from more, messed with her head.

She leaned forward and told me, "I think you hired me because you were always worried that an out-of-family therapist will have to break their confidentiality and report to authorities, knowing about the terrible things Deji's done back home, but never told you about."

3

The running water from the bathroom suddenly stopped, and I shook my head as if to rid myself of my encounter with Katherine.

I pinched my cheeks and steadied up against the bed's frame, and then turned on Deji's favorite incandescent lights by the nightstand. The room became swathed in warm light.

My husband's six-foot athletic frame stood half-naked by the bathroom door, a towel around his waist. He hadn't dried his face yet, so traces of his tears would go unnoticed. I knew him too well.

"Wanna grab a bite, Snowflake?" I said in a chirpy voice, "I can heat up that pizza from yesterday."

He smiled with his sweet white teeth because I called him snowflake. He never quite liked the name but never objected. Katherine claimed I called him that to delude myself into him being someone lovable and evade his true darker nature.

I called him Snowflake because I was the paler one, so it instead felt paradoxically funny to me. The irony alone made me chuckle, and Deji went along with it.

"Why pizza?" He jumped into bed, leaned his head against my thighs, and looked into my eyes. "You're delicious and salty enough."

It was moments like these that made me remember Katherine. I never wanted anything in the world but Deji and Andrew. And I had them both. It was good—more than I could ask for.

But these sentimental moments were as scary as sweet because what if they were gone tomorrow? What if someone took the precious things that kept me going and left me undone? It was uncanny how I couldn't shake the feeling.

Emma always claimed I was one who practiced self-sabotage by feeling they didn't deserve their lives. In all honesty, this wasn't what scared me. Somewhere deep inside, I feared that Katherine was right about Deji.

"You're sure you don't want to eat before sleep?"

"Nah, but thanks," he said. "I'm taking Andrew to see the Arsenal game in London tomorrow. I better sleep early."

"Okay," I said, appreciating his goodnight smile.

His teeth glimmered in the low-lit room. I thought it was that smile that I first noticed about him when we first met. I could never imagine me falling for him then. Every girl in my family married a British boy, except my cousin, who found herself a man of Viking descent while studying abroad.

It was Deji's dimples that made me fall for him. He had a peculiar smile. Not only beautiful, but he wanted to smile, even though you could see the bitterness of his childhood in the slight slopes at the sides of his lips.

Looking at him now also reminded me of my father. Deji worked for him at some point, assisting him with moving paintings as he traveled to offer them in exhibitions. Deji studied to become a fitness instructor, which he succeeded at. It was our primary source for paying the bills. He was happy to fulfill the traditional family role of being the provider.

"Come to papa," he intentionally said in his Najimbian accent and slid under the sheets and embraced me from behind. I laced my hands into him as I felt his breath on my neck.

"Can I ask you a favor?' I said.

"I promise I won't work out early in the morning. Tomorrow is

Andrew's day. So, I'll postpone it until the evening."

"It's not that. Would you please drive Andrew to the football match and not take the train?"

"I could, but he loves the train."

I sighed. Andrew really loved trains. His favorite nursery rhyme was about trains. Somehow, he didn't like most of the children's songs I tried to get him into. But once I told him about the Choo Choo train, he couldn't stop singing it. Even more, he started to become obsessed with trains. Be it Lego or on TV. Something about trains just resonated with him.

"I know," I said. "It's just that some kid disappeared on the same train to London a few days ago. "

"That's terrible. How didn't I hear about it?"

"You don't watch the news, remember?" I nudged him. "You think it's all fabricated lies and all fear-mongering for the sake of the dirty greens."

"I'll never change my mind. You know they lie about what's happening back in my home country every day. Those wars, the killings, and poverty could've been all stopped, hadn't they escalated every little mishap to unreal proportions to hide the fact that they want the oil and natural resources in our land."

I didn't know what to say. What hadn't been said before anyway? If I commented, it would lead to me asking about what happened to him there before he arrived in the UK at the age of six. He just turned thirty and looking that far back wasn't worth it to weaken the strength of our marriage.

"Tell me about the kid on the train," he said inquisitively.

"He just vanished in thin air. He left his house and kissed his mum goodbye to attend a course in London. He never arrived in London. Never came back. Last he was spotted on CCTV getting on the train. It's as if it swallowed him whole." Even I could hear the tinge of fear in my voice.

Deji squeezed my fingers, "Okay, I'll tell Andrew that the view from Dorchester to London is better from the car and that we could eat ice cream from the best shop that can only be reached halfway."

"Thanks, babe," I squeezed his hand back, grateful for his under-standing.

I was happy and relieved he took me seriously. This felt too good, the understanding and hand-holding. And though it was all that mattered, I still couldn't shake that feeling away. The feeling that Deji was keeping something from me.

Minutes later, Andrew entered the room, unable to sleep. As a six-year-old, he was a little too old for that by American standards. But Deji still liked to spoil him and squeezed him into the bed between us. Andrew hugged him and smiled as he cuddled his little body closer to Deji.

I could've used a hug myself, but sometimes I felt Andrew was too attached to his father. Katherine hinted at it more than once, espe-cially when she felt the need to bring me down. But I let it slide. I wasn't going to be that insecure and whiney mother after all.

I wrapped my arms around Andrew from behind, and the three of us started to drift off to sleep. Then, to please my son and wonder if he wanted to hug me back, I hummed his favorite Choo Choo train rhyme in his ears.

It worked.

Andrew turned around and hugged me, though his eyes were closed. He'd fallen into sleep already.

I wish he looked at me that night so I could've stared into these eyes for one last time.

4

My father used to say that reality was so harsh that it couldn't be lived without denial — at least for a while. That was why he took painting as a profession. It made little money but made a lot of sense as it was a great escape. An escape he taught me that I found to be more important than money.

Whatever the customer paid him for his art was good money because he'd already paid himself with peace of mind. Art was escapism. It made him feel high. It made him tolerate my mother and remind him that he once loved her and that she gave him the greatest gift of all: me.

Still, once in a while, Snowflake, he used to say, *life will hit you a bit too harshly no art can heal you for some time. The secret is not to heal but to understand it is not your fault.*

Experiencing the day after Deji promised me not to take the train had to be my fault. It was the weekend, and I'd slept for too long, unaware when Deji and Andrew woke up and left for the game.

Groggily, I woke up, brushed my teeth, and washed, then went to the kitchen for coffee. I was going to check my phone because Deji usually kept me up to date about his travels. As I reached for it on the counter, my eyes darted to the television. What I saw on the TV screen forced me to stop.

The TV showed a train, just as I had feared, and some headlines about missing persons. But it was on mute. Deji always left it on mute as he thought no one watched TV anymore except for YouTube, and if they did, it would be on a phone or laptop.

I was old-fashioned, honoring my father's memory for always leaving the TV open while working. I celebrated my father in all possible ways, just like I called Deji Snowflake because my father used to call me that. I guess I loved Deji that much.

Reading the headlines on the muted TV didn't make much sense to me. The mind always saw — and read — what it wanted to, not what was factual and objective. I thought this was about the poor boy who disappeared on the train a few days ago, so I went to grab the remote control and unmute the TV. My heart pounded in my chest as I tried to ignore every woman's instinct.

My legs wouldn't let me make my way to the remote. My body knew what was going on while my mind resisted it.

Wait a minute, I thought to myself. *What am I worried about?* I tried to rationalize with logic to outweigh the pull of intuition.

Yes, I realized the date on the muted TV was today. Yes, I realized this was about the train from Dorchester to London. And yes, I read the words' *possible terrorist attack*' on the headliner at the bottom of the screen.

But no, I refused to comprehend.

I refused to believe this would happen to me. I mean, this stuff happened to other people on TV. We were supposed to sympathize, pat them on the shoulder, and help them cope.

But this stuff never happened to us, right?

I wiped my itchy eyes, unsure what was going on with them. Why were my legs cemented in place? Why was my heart pounding faster, as if it would leap from my chest?

The headline at the bottom added another phrase: *nine people kidnapped.*

My eyes itched again. I thought I had some stress reflex. Was I getting sick? Why couldn't I move?

I took a breath and then a few steps, only I walked toward our third-story window in the opposite direction of the remote. My legs wanted me to look outside. I began panting. My eyes itched more — a cold sweat starting on my forehead. My heart dropped to my toes, and my eyes widened.

What the fuck is outside my window?

And there I stopped, looking down at the parking lot of our apartment, staring at Deji's car.

At that moment, I realized what the itching in my eyes was. I was weeping in silence—thick, slow, and viscous tears without a shriek or a scream.

I began to panic and ran back to the TV.

My body knew that I'd collapse within the next few seconds, and my mind and heart needed to know what happened before I gave in to the shock.

Nine people were kidnapped in the terrorist attack that occurred on the train earlier this morning. A Caucasian mother and daughter, two Indian sisters, the train conductor, a toddler, the man they shot when he tried to resist, and an African man and his son. We will have more to report

The broadcaster's voice began to fade, as did everything around me as I realized without a doubt that Deji lied to me and still took the train with Andrew.

It was my fault. Why didn't I wake up early enough to ensure they wouldn't?

5

THREE MONTHS AGO...

"I didn't mean to interfere, but I appreciate you're talking to me," Jason Ross said across the table in that outdoor restaurant he suggested.

Commonly, I wouldn't have accepted the invitation, but he felt like a sign from the stars to me. Was Emma rubbing off on me a bit? The day I decided to move on, I met him. Emma's texts confirmed she was elated, and she agreed that our encounter on the train was destiny, but I could not entertain her long. I had more pressing matters at hand.

What if he knew something about what happened? And if he didn't, why would I have objected to talking to someone who experienced the same pain?

I mean, Katherine never really understood me. For the past eight years, she borderline pushed me into dating and living my life as if nothing had happened. I was thirty-six now, and not even my best friend Emma had filled that void left by my son and husband.

"How haven't we met before?" I asked Jason, almost unsympathetically. I treated him as a source for my resolution, I guess. Sometimes, when I reminded myself, I felt like I was the wrong person in so many ways, trying to point fingers at others.

Jason shrugged. He was too good-looking for a man in his early forties. Too good looking for a man who was suffering. Or was he?

He leaned back and let the barista deliver our drinks. He ordered a latte with strawberry flavor, which I hadn't heard of before. He explained that he had severe allergies to almonds and hazelnut. Whenever he ordered a non-flavored latte, the baristas usually made a mistake and still put some flavor. The easiest way to overcome his dilemma was to order strawberries, so they had no choice.

I ordered the same as a courtesy. I wasn't here to drink a latte but to gather knowledge. We both nursed our hot beverages in silence, working up the nerve to find the words.

"I didn't want to meet you," he finally spoke. It was a fractured voice. I felt the same after the incident. Someone would want to talk about it with me, and my mind would go blank, my soul black, and my voice would be shattered into splintered inside of me, cutting through the fabric of strength I pretended I still had.

"I understand," I said. "I didn't want to meet anyone associated with the tragedy. The pain was too great. I was told it would help the healing process, but I never believed it. I only met with the conductor's family and the man who resisted because I thought it was brave."

"Edward Kosinski, that was his name," Jason nodded.

"Yes, true," I was impressed he remembered it so vividly. I had long forced it out of my mind out of survival.

"He resisted because he was a police officer. Not his shift, but he felt obligated. The terrorist didn't want him. They wanted the others."

"Are you suggesting the terrorists picked my son and husband on purpose?"

"No one ever knew, but I think there was a picking process," Jason said. "I mean Pakistani terrorists kidnapping passengers on a train to bargain with the government for other terrorists in British custody; that might make sense, but why pick these nine individuals?"

"They needed hostages to trade," I replied, a sentence I told myself repeatedly inside my mind through the years. "And since the government never complied, our loved ones were forever gone."

"You see, there are so many things about that day that trouble me about this story," He leaned forward, almost whispering. I realized that he treated me likewise, a source of knowledge. He thought I might know something. We were two lost souls, hanging on straws with a common connection and need to find answers from our tragic pasts.

"I mean, a Pakistani terrorist taking hostages like my wife and daughter, I can believe that, but your husband? No."

"What's different about my husband?"

"Don't take it the wrong way, but I work with immigrants in my line of work. A Pakistani will side with the African man. Minorities stood by minorities," he said. "Again, I don't mean anything by that. It's just what I know."

"What's your line of work?"

He leaned back, probably not liking my interrogating demeanor. Nevertheless, his retreat only heightened my curious nature.

"I work for Welcome Home Inc.," he sighed. "You know it?"

"Of course. Ads are everywhere. You help immigrants live and establish a better life in first-world countries. My husband liked your services a lot, but you rejected his application," I wanted to be suspicious about such a coincidence, but like my hunch about the train Deji and Andrew took, I had no concrete basis or grounds to rely on.

"It's a big company. It rejects most applicants."

"But it pays well, I assume," I said.

"Hence the Rolex watch and Armani suits," he pointed at himself, slightly irritated. Was that sincere? "I joined this line of work to help people but then realized it's a business like any other."

"Look, Mr. Ross," I gently rapped a hand on the table. "I'm not so sure that this was a good idea. We're two lost people trying to hang on to a past that we may never figure out. I've tried it all. Hired private detectives, pressured the police, and attempted to find my son and husband — or know what happened to them. All I know is one thing,"

"Which is?"

"They're statistically dead."

"I suppose the police told you that."

"I did my research," I said, leaning forward and locking eyes with him. "I studied the past. Unfortunately, no one ever returned from a similar kidnapping. Over ninety percent of the terrorist attacks have no concrete resolution."

Jason shrugged and nodded, touching the rim of his glass again. Neither of us sipped the latte anymore. We just held the mugs in our hands as if to give them something to do. It was nothing but social lubrication, trying to pretend we were all right when we were holding on by a thread. Something I was a professional at now.

"I'm sorry if I've pushed you," he said. "Please understand that I did the same. I've contacted you today because..." he swallowed the words midway, and I found him rather sincere again.

Something inside me didn't want me to feel that way, but I couldn't help myself. Then again, I didn't have conversations with many people throughout these past few years.

My father used to say that artists were introverts, self-sabotaging themselves with the delusional beauty of creation.

"Never mind," he said. "Anyway, I ran through the same pain you've been through. I've only found it a weird coincidence that both our spouses were immigrants."

It seemed like a genuine remark, even though I wasn't sure about it — I've never checked the other passengers' backgrounds.

I wanted to comfort him and say something, but I understood that this was just another flicker of suspicions about something we couldn't prove. An open door to hell disguised as a pathway to hope.

True, I met with him to see if he knew something. By something, I meant a substantial piece of information, not a sliver of speculation. Had he even told me a concrete method to cope with losing my loved ones, I'd have listened to him.

"I'll order the check," he said, "thank you for agreeing to have coffee with me. I appreciate it. I really do."

I nodded, appreciating him as well. There was something about him that I liked but also didn't.

As I said, I've always been a paradox of emotions and decisions. He needed to understand that I'd been through this for eight years, so much so that people around me sometimes thought I went cold and stopped thinking about it. After so many years, I realized I had only so many tears to cry, so many crazy and lonely nights praying — then cursing. So many days, I went down the alcohol route and was snatched out of it by Emma. For so many years, I was gulping medicine and chewing on pills, doing anything I could to numb the pain.

There was a time in the beginning when I had terrible thoughts whenever I was alone, and I was alone a lot.

I couldn't enjoy balconies because something told me to jump. I preferred to be away from the kitchen and ordered only delivery food because I was better off away from knives and sharp objects. I showered instead of taking baths for fear of succumbing to staying under the water, never coming back up for a breath.

I wasn't sure how Jason coped, but I was a mess, and I wasn't proud. Had anyone asked me what really bothered me, I'd have told them: I couldn't tolerate not knowing how I should feel and the constant plague of unanswered questions that swirled in my mind.

Did my son and husband die? Were they kidnapped? And if so, did that mean they were tortured? Why did the police seem to hide something? What was I supposed to do about that but scream and curse — all the reactions that made things worse? And what was I supposed to do about the government and media involvement?

Terrorist attacks were situations where people weren't treated as individuals. Some hateful group hurts a bunch of innocent people. It was always a bunch. It was always the plural victims, not the singular individual.

Besides, and I didn't want to think much of it then, I sensed there was negligence toward my husband being kidnapped. Several times the police addressed me as, 'Ah, she is the African's wife.' Time and time again, I had to remind them that it wasn't just my husband who'd been kidnapped but also my son.

"I don't suppose exchanging phone numbers is a good idea," he said as he stood up, picking up his Armani jacket, probably returning to his Welcome Home Inc.

"Why not?" I pulled out my phone. I didn't see the objection, or maybe something inside me wanted to keep that thread open.

We exchanged phone numbers and paid for drinks we didn't have, the same way we paid for sins we didn't commit in this life.

Before we parted, I had to ask, "Can I ask why you decided to contact me today?"

"Well, it's a personal thing that I thought would be too much of a giveaway," Jason shrugged again, his body half tilted in the opposite direction where he was head, "I think it's ridiculous."

"Try me," oh, boy, how insistent a mother could get when her instincts told her to follow one of those pathways to hell.

"I promised myself to look for my family for eight years — don't ask me why," he now tucked his hands in his pockets and sighed. "Today is the day I decided to move on."

6

The week after our encounter on the train, I couldn't stop thinking about Jason. I was fully aware that I was lonely and that he was attractive. We shared a dangerously emotional connection of traumatic pain that we seemed to bond over — never mind how I acted off-putting. My actions were my futile attempt to mask my true feelings that bubbled to the surface each time I thought of him.

The feelings of attraction were not the only reason why I kept thinking about him. It was an uncanny coincidence that he decided to *move on* the same day I did. Emma would say there was no such thing as coincidences. I, too, must admit it was quite strange.

Had this been a novel, I'd predicted what happened next. The two protagonists would fall in love and heal each other's pain, then have children and live happily ever after while honoring their lost ones. As if it were that simple in reality.

Books had a funny way of handling things in a predictable yet pleasant manner. They were words, after all. How was I expected to give into and trust words when I could not describe my complex and interconnected feelings in those exact words. My father used to say that a painter's brush had the upper hand over words because of the flexibility of reinterpretation. A painting oozed with many emotions and meaning, depending on where you glanced or even how much older you've become looking at them again.

Words, on the other hand, were fixed. They were supposed to translate a feeling that in and of itself couldn't be accurately described in the first place.

I hadn't told anyone that I had decided to move on that day. I hadn't even hinted at it. Not to Katherine, not to Emma – despite her encouragement, not even to the support groups that I attended every now and then when I needed to know that I wasn't suffering alone. That I wasn't a Snowflake of misery all by myself.

So it was just a coincidence? Why would he use the same choice of words? Why not say 'I gave up' or 'I stopped looking' or something cheesy like 'my wife and daughter would've wanted me to stop looking'? These were the questions I pondered in between grander notions of thinking about Jason himself.

Instead of finishing my painting of African children for a charity organization — don't get me wrong, they still paid me — that Emma had hooked me up with, I stalked Jason online.

There wasn't much about him. His social media profiles were private. His pictures were few. Headshots of a handsome man in a suit and a blondish, almost boyish haircut. The Rolex watch and corporate smile. He came off as someone I wouldn't like based on the pictures. A businessman whose smile was insincere and only shined under a camera flash. His whole presence and attitude served his career just about right.

There were no articles about him as an individual. He didn't seem like a CEO or someone at the top of the hierarchy. Just a well-paid man, sticking to the script. Photos of his colleagues where he stood second row because of his height were also few. Again, all business, all cringe-worthy for an artist like me. I found it too sterile an environment for my creative mind. He practically hung out with the type of people I ran from when I left my family.

Most pictures showed the initials W.H. in the back somewhere. Welcome Home's logo. It was as if he didn't have a personal life. But then again, who was I to judge. You hardly found pictures of me online. I hated it. Still, I worried. I had two reasons.

One: for a corporation that helped immigrants enjoy a better life in first-world countries, not one of the pics showed him with an actual immigrant or client, for that matter. On the contrary, all Welcome Home's photos on their website were of immigrants from all over the world, intertwined with the employee that handled their case. They told success stories and offered testimonials left and right, praising the company's efforts, and mentioning several of the employees by name.

But not Jason. He worked there but never mingled with their clients? I could understand camera shy for privacy reasons, but not even a review mentioning him?

I didn't have an answer to this. My left brain suggested that he was in the office work and could have had no access to the immigrants themselves. However, my right brain didn't like this at all. It seemed too suspicious for my inquisitive nature.

Two: this is the part that I cared more about. I couldn't find a picture of his daughter or wife. Not anywhere. Worse, no mention of their names before or after the train incident. This sent red flags and warning sirens through my mind. Maybe I wasn't looking hard enough?

It bothered me so much that I went to Andrew's room, where I had shoved a box of papers under his bed, hidden away from mind and sight to avoid an emotional confrontation. It was full of documentation I received about the train investigations that I had saved all these years. Police reports, interrogations transcripts, and pieces of news here and there.

I hadn't opened it in four years. That was when I'd lost faith in the official investigating channel and began to dig deeper on my own, desperate to find an answer.

Now a tug in my heart beckoned me to open it. I thought it'd only take a minute but opening the door to Andrew's room took my breath away. I suddenly realized I hadn't been back up here in four years. Had time really passed that quickly? For the first four years, I saw the room where Andrew had slept, played, and enjoyed. I used to clean it up myself, putting away the endless toy trains. I used to sleep on the top bunk of his bunk bed to keep him company — Deji always thought we would give him a sister, but we realized it'd be too much expense. I used to be so present in this room, living the life of a doting mother.

After the incident, I used to sleep in his bed in a fetal position and cry. When I realized that crying didn't bother me as much as wanting to hug him and sing to him, I began to embrace his toys and teddy bears. I felt an automatic pull to step away from the memories of Andrew, of our family. I was about to close the door again when I took a deep breath and reminded myself of the pathway to hell. I needed strength to stop myself from wallowing in the harsh reminders, hoping they would shed insight on my recent questions about Jason's family.

On my knees, I pulled the box from under the bed and checked the police reports scanning and reading carefully looking for anything that would indicate an answer. A little later, I sat crossed-legged, trying not to look left or right for fear my emotions would betray me. Not looking at the walls with Andrew's charcoal drawings, not at his closet, and not the window we shared when it got gloomy and rainy outside, but we were happy with glee to be cozy and dry together inside.

My eyes stuck to the documents, for my need for answers was stronger than the memories pulling at my heart. I was looking to see whether this Jason Ross I met had his name in any reports. After about an hour of digging in the large stack of papers, I finally found it. There was even a picture of him.

He was listed as the husband of Natalie Novokov, and father of Mila, no last name was given. The newspaper had included a family photo of the three under the headline: *Local Father Loses Family in Terrorist Tragedy.*

Oh, boy, how cute his daughter was, so happy too. Ten-years-old. I sighed. She was so young.

Fuck me. I'm not a special snowflake. How could I pretend I was the only one with unjust done to them?

I couldn't help but notice Natalie being a lawyer. I didn't know why but I didn't expect that based on her appearance in the photo. She seemed free-spirited, not the corporate type. Upon closer inspection of the article, it appeared that she worked for Welcome Home as well. Happy with my discovery, I stood up and hurried back to the computer and googled her name. There she was, all shiny all over the internet. She had many followers on every social media app. She had a cooking show that was non-profit. She and her daughter cooked for Russian housewives. Mila shone brightly in every video.

This was a happy family, stolen by a few angry extremists while on a train, thinking this wasn't the last day of their lives — normal lives at least.

I wasn't surprised Natalie took a train instead of that Austin Martin that showed up in some of her pictures. She came off as down to earth, and unlike Jason, she was a borderline celebrity in the immigration world of Welcome Home. Pictures of her with immigrants — mostly Russians — were all over the internet. An activist, philanthropist, and even an investor. I suspected she made more money than Jason. Actually, that had to be the case with her success in multiple arenas.

Her job title and cause made more sense to me. She fought for immigrant rights and wished to better the laws. She also helped them get citizenship and cut ties with their older issues in their homeland. I didn't quite know what the latter part meant precisely, but I could only assume it was to help her image in Western Society.

I spent hours stalking her life — I mean past life. As they say, I fell down the internet's rabbit hole trying to learn everything I could about her. I only stopped when I realized that she had left Welcome Home a year before her kidnapping. That was the year when she started her cooking class online. Did she not practice anymore? That part was vague and sudden.

Also, after hours of surfing the web, there wasn't one picture of her and Jason as a family. Only a couple of pictures posing second row with their team members in career-driven, propaganda pictures for Welcome Home. They stood far from each other. No hint of them having been an item. If I hadn't met Jason or uncovered the newspaper article, I'd never assumed they had a daughter together, let alone were married.

Mila's many social profiles had no pictures of Jason either. I tried to read comments, fetching anything about her being married, but I found none. Now, this was suspicious. Even if you want to maintain professionalism in the office, which could explain the distance between them in the Welcome Home photos, wouldn't you have at least one picture of your so-called husband on your personal pages?

Stop it, Kate. I could hear my father's voice now. *When was 'moving on' a synonym for prying into other people's lives?*

It wasn't like Kyle Mason, my father, was convincing this time, but I still took his words to heart. Knowing that I needed the support from him, even if it was just in my mind, to be firm in my decision to move on.

Rest in peace, Picasso — that was what I called him sometimes. I should stick to the plan and move on. And you know what? I'll erase Jason's number, too. There's no sense going on a wild goose chase when I just decided to start my life anew.

That was when my eyes caught that image of Natalie Novokov in the lower right corner of the Google image search page. That was when I felt that clutch in my heart again. I knew that I was about to open all the doors to hell and stare right into the abyss.

The picture was of Natalie in some expensive dinner gathering at what looked like one of London's elite parties. She held out a champagne glass with hands embracing a woman called Katherine King.

7

Andrew never liked Katherine.

Not that he ever vocalized it or complained about her. He was too young to care, treading all over the apartment as if he were a light feather of joy and curiosity. Whenever in Katherine's proximity, he looked worried to me, guarded, as if he knew deep down or instinctual she was not to be trusted.

I remember wondering if it was because of me. My disdain for my mother wasn't a secret, but I tried my best not to show it publicly, especially for my own family's sake. Yes, I despised her, but it wasn't enough reason to deny her spending time with Andrew under my watchful eyes.

I never told anyone what she had done to my father except Deji. Andrew never met his grandfather, yet eerily enough went to touch his picture, which I hung in my painting room.

That could've been it, but every once in a while, Andrew's curiosity would lead him into the room, eager to learn more about him. For a six-year-old who rarely asked about others, it always caught me by surprise in a most pleasant way.

Deji later suggested I'd hang Katherine's photo, so our son wouldn't grow up consumed with ideas about broken families or have tainted views of Katherine. Deji preferred for Andrew to surmise his own conclusions on the adults in his life when he was old enough to make that choice instead of directly seeing our own favoring one parent over the other.

Reluctantly, I did. But whenever my artistic flow was blocked, and I was out of ideas, I draped Katherine's picture in a white blanket, and hooray, I felt creative again. It's almost as if her negative energy sucked the very life out of me, even through her photograph.

"Maybe invite Katherine to Andrew's sixth birthday," Emma told me once, sitting on a bench in the park on one of Dorchester's few sunny days.

We were eating our favorite Kalachi Sandwich from a small standing parlor in London. Emma hadn't moved to London then, but whenever I sold a painting to Londoners, we took a trip to celebrate. Deji had introduced me to this place. Najimbian food at its delicious, carb-infested, greasy-soaked finest. It puzzled me how Deji ate this and stayed fit.

"Why this year when I never invited her before?" I told her.

"It's just a suggestion," she said, running her hands through her blonde hair. We both had almost the same hair in color and feel. She let it run long while I trimmed it shorter than shoulder length. It was either this, or my hair got stained with paint while working for hours — it was a hassle to clean it up. "I mean, we both know Deji's family is in Najimbia, and that Andrew will never get to see them, so at least make him get in touch with yours."

"Mine is only Katherine. Had dad been alive, I'd have welcomed this connection."

"As good as it gets, Kate. One day you'll have to explain to Andrew the unexplainable. Why his dad came here alone and lived in an orphanage for most of his life. That his mother died in the process of getting him out of a war-infested country where kids were handed guns to fight one another. In my opinion, Andrew needs Katherine."

"Why is everyone treating me as if Katherine is the good one and I'm the bad daughter," I stopped eating.

"Whoa," she laughed, "defensive much?"

"I guess so. First, Deji asks me to hang Katherine's picture, and then you want me to invite her. I assume the next thing you were about to say was that Andrew needs to get to know her better and that I should send him to visit her in her mansion."

"Why not?" she ate with passion as if my attitude didn't affect her in the slightest.

Emma enjoyed everything to the max. Indulgence was her middle name, be it a sandwich, a movie, or a man. That's why she stayed single, she said, because every man had an expiration date to their enjoyment. Being twenty-six, unwed, and childless offered her that independent freedom I couldn't wrap my head around. She said, "Being a mother is a job. Part of it is to connect your son to his roots."

"Says the girl who might never marry or have kids," I rolled my eyes and tried my best to mirror her lust for food.

"I didn't take the job, remember?" she snickered. "You signed the papers and took an oath," she lowered the sandwich and raised one hand in the air, "Dear Judge, may I latch myself to this man forever and ever and live miserable ever after?"

I laughed and nudged her, "Deji makes me happy. You're jealous."

"I am," she said, and she meant it. "You landed a man who is actually a man. That's why Kyle called you a Snowflake."

"You only met Kyle a year before he died, yet you quote him all the time. I'm impressed."

"You, Kate Mason, are oblivious of the gift you have. Maybe you're miserable with your mother, but you landed two good men in your life at once. A father and husband."

"And a son!"

"Oh," she raised an eyebrow. "I forgot about him. Well, he isn't a man yet, but he is a stunner. With all that brown skin and blonde hair, and blue eyes, girls will go nuts for him."

"So you think I should invite Katherine?" I said, considering the consequences of her visiting us in our humble apartment on the third floor in a middle-class housing area. Cringing at the expected insults from Katherine about the state of our living conditions. Not that we were impoverished, but middle-class living is a big step down from infinite wealth, and well, Katherine always seems to make sure we didn't forget.

"Not just Katherine," Emma faced me with eyes open wide, "Doctor, Psychologist, Ph.D., renowned, rich ass bitch, Katherine King!" she said mockingly.

I couldn't stop laughing.

Two days later, and a week before the train incident, we hosted Andrew's sixth birthday in our apartment. Regretfully, I invited Katherine.

Not only did she arrive with a couple of her snobby friends whom I'd never seen before, but she wouldn't stop belittling our apartment and my husband, which was what I expected from her.

"That's my daughter, Kate Mason," she told her two friends. "She isn't as poor as she looks. It's an artistic choice."

I swallowed my urges to stand up for my family in front of these snobby strangers, yet held back and kept silent, not wanting to ruin Andrew's birthday. From the corner of my eyes, I saw Deji omitting a smile as if he was saying, 'hold on, Snowflake, and let the storm pass.' He knew me through and through.

As for Deji, he avoided her like the plague, despite the fact that Katherine managed to always find a way to keep him in arm's reach. Never did her conversation with him avoid the subject matter of how strong and fit of an African man he was.

"My friends absolutely drool over that sexy species of your husband when they see his videos on YouTube," she said to me. Of course, she made sure to say this within earshot of her so-called friends to entertain them with my discomfort. These two ladies were buried in jewelry that magically couldn't make them look any younger and chuckled lightly like schoolgirls at the boldness of Katherine's comment.

"I feel like I'm in that movie 'Get Out,'" Deji hissed to me a minute later while we arranged plates to prepare for the birthday cake.

"Are you sure your mother won't kill me and take my soul and put it in one of those old women?"

"You're the one who says she is a good psychiatrist," I teased him.

It always puzzled me how he liked her as a psychiatrist but not as a human being. Even now, he mentioned that she was brilliant in her job.

"You know what kind of psychiatrist she is?" he said, eyeing her across the living room as she was trying to hug Andrew. "The kind which, though brilliant, needs a psychiatrist."

"Well said," I agreed. "I'll never understand why everyone thinks she is so good at her job. On the other hand, maybe that's why dad liked her." Deji tilted his head toward me and gave me that attractively teasing look, "You're not scheming with your mother on this, are you?"

"What do you mean?" I chuckled because I liked it when he made that face. It was as if we were not lovers but little kids in the playground playing tag.

"In that 'Get Out' movie, the white girl brought in her black fiancé to offer his soul to her family."

"Stop it," I hit him in the chest, my eyes drifting sideways if anyone heard him. Deji never shied away from saying white, black, and so on. He wasn't part of the reserved society around us that coveted words and pretended racism didn't exist. If it was unjust, it was unfair. No sugar coating, direct honesty, all while he never generalized. Not all types of a particular ethnicity were good or bad. He welcomed everyone until proven otherwise.

He pulled me closer and kissed me. I pulled back out of embarrassment with everyone around us not wanting to give Katherine and her 'friends' something else to drool over.

"What are you doing?" I mouthed to him with glaring eyes.

"I was testing whether your mouth told me lies," he winked. "It turns out you're an open book, Kate Mason."

Our flirtatious moment was then interrupted by Andrew calling my name, attempting to free himself from Katherine. She had him firmly in between her hands, and he pushed her away. It was a hard job balancing out the conflict. I stood by Andrew's choice but knew Deji would want peace. Convincing Katherine that he was still grateful for her attendance and care while still making sure Andrew wasn't upset over the encounter.

Later that night, I combed his hair and asked him, "Why do you always call out for me when you want to escape grandma? I mean, you usually call dad for help."

It was selfish to ask him, but I was curious. Was I doing something right, wrong, or what? Deji was Andrew's solace at all times. He even asked him to stop that neighbor's kid, who was a bully, from hurting his other friends one time. Deji was almost Andrew's bodyguard. When it came to Katherine, he asked for my help, not Deji's.

"Dad can't help with grandmother," Andrew said, looking in the mirror, eyes focused with concern only for his curly hair. "He is afraid of her."

8

THREE MONTHS AGO...

"Oh, Natalie, she was a charmer," Katherine said on the phone, indicating her fondness for an old colleague. "I think she was kidnapped on the same train, right?"

Katherine never shied away from talking about the train. I don't think I'd ever seen her mourn my husband and son. I tried to catch my breath and collect my thoughts before asking more questions. My thoughts were scattered already, and I had to take a breath to regain my focus.

"How come I've never heard about her before?"

"How come you've heard about her now?" Katherine's investigative psychologist's voice resonated in my ears.

I didn't want to tell her about my meeting with Jason. I wasn't sure why, but I could not stand that she met my question with another question.

"I was looking through the victim names from the incidents and came across her name."

"You came across her name years ago when you also ran through every name," Katherine said. "It's rather odd that you act as if you've never read her name before."

She was right about this, but I needed her to confess to knowing someone else tied to the tragedy. Someone who she worked with yet never brought it up before.

Since meeting Jason, I began to think that I'd been a little selfish about how I handled questions about the train in the past. And though most of it was all a blur and haze now, I was never interested in the other passengers. Sure, I remember going through the names, wanting to see if there was a connection or anything, but come to think of it now, I couldn't even remember the name of the man who resisted the terrorists — and I was most interested in him after Deji and Andrew.

"Kate?" Katherine said. "Are you still there?"

"I'm not calling for you to refresh my memory, Katherine," I countered. "I wonder how you two met?"

"Like I meet anyone. A dinner party, or social interactions within the exclusive circle I tend to keep."

"What does that mean?"

Katherine sighed, "She was rich, Kate, one of the elites. I wined and dined with them all the time."

It rang true and convincing. Natalie and Jason were the perfect candidates to run into Katherine through social life. Yet I couldn't help but feel that something felt wrong again.

Katherine rarely talked about herself this way. Whenever I criticized the shallow rich life she led in the past, she was the first one to defend it. Katherine made sure to tell me about all the good things the rich did for the poor and were never thanked for. She never belittled herself talking about her life like that, not even close.

"She did business with you, didn't she?".

Katherine said nothing for some time, seemingly weighing her words in her mind carefully before allowing her voice to take hold of them.

"Mother?" I was fully aware of my choice to call her mother. I wanted her to warm up a little and tell me the truth if that was even possible with her. I betrayed myself a little and broke down the wall I had built in the promise I would never call her that again. It was emotional blackmail on my end when it would give me the answers I needed. It was Katherine we were talking about here, queen of emotional blackmail.

"Natalie was a lawyer," Katherine began. "She defended immigrants mostly. God bless her; she had a cause and stood by it. Part of this was getting the best psychological evaluation for her clients. That's where I fit in. I did it for free, by the way."

"I'm not sure I understand her job yet. Why did immigrants need evaluations?"

"A lot of them were like Deji, Kate. Coming from troubled pasts and trauma-filled lives. Why did you think I persuaded you to let me be his psychiatrist?"

"I thought you wanted to help. According to you, you wanted to know about anything he may have done in the past." I said, making sure to remind her of her own words.

I was utterly lost to what this conversation was about. I never believed Deji did something terrible, and I wasn't talking to her to know about him. I wanted to know about Natalie. Katherine did have a way of skirting around the issue.

"Could you ever make things easier for both of us and tell me in plain English what you did for Natalie?" I asked, attempting to hide my frustrations with her.

"Could you keep your mouth shut if I told you what you needed to know?"

I nodded and shrugged, but I didn't utter a word. I knew she could tell whether I agreed or not through the silence I offered her on my end of the phone. Because whether I liked to admit it or not, she was still my mother. Mothers had a way of knowing their daughters through all things and could pick up on the hidden clues silence brought them.

"Immigrants, especially in their first years, are treated with discrete scrutiny by the government. Of course, you will never hear this in public," she began. "So when lawyers like Natalie fight for the immigrant's right to have a better life and chances to grow as a person in first world countries, the government needs psychological evaluations about their behavior. That's where I came in. Natalie only took good immigrants or refugees under her wings. In her valiant effort to speed up the process of them settling down and living a good life, instead of the alternative of being thrown to less than minimum wage living and such things, she sent them to me. I wrote the reports she needed to allow this to happen."

"But examined them first, right?"

"When will you ever grow up and live in the real world, Kate?" She grunted. It reminded me of how she taunted me in my childhood. "No, I didn't have a chance to clear my conscience and make an indisputable assessment whether they were — and were going to — stay good citizens. Firstly, because psychology isn't really a science. We want to believe we know people by studying them, writing books, and finding patterns, but it's never without a doubt."

She was borderline yelling at me, and I didn't have an indisputable assessment of why she felt the need to do this.

"And the second reason?"

"Because most of them are fucked up," she was indisputably yelling at me now, leaning on the loudness of her voice to get her through the pain of revealing the truth. "Most of them have embraced darkness wherever they came from. Natalie knew that too, and we bonded over doing our best to find a balance, by her investigating and giving a chance to those who needed it the most."

"And Deji was part of this?"

"Yes," she strangely lowered her voice and let out a longer sigh as if she were meditating or something. "But Natalie had nothing to do with him. Deji arrived when he was six years old, and he was raised here. He is who the government considered least likely to be a threat or violent or have suicidal tendencies himself. And before you ask, I will never disclose with you what he told me about his childhood."

I hated that I pressured her but liked the fact that she came across as human for once. It was rare to hear Katherine being passionate about something. I hadn't grasped all of this, needing a moment to digest the new information she brought to me., Although I wanted to thank her again, I found that I couldn't utter the words of gratitude when my father's image flashed before my eyes.

I asked her one last thing, "None of this web of secrets and coincidences about Natalie, Deji, and you would have to do with what happened, not the train, right?"

"Of course not," Katherine said. "But…"

"Yes?" I questioned, doing my best to hide the fear in my voice.

"But I keep asking myself if the terrorists were ever someone I wrote a good report for. Someone I shouldn't have let in but did in good faith and my rush to assist Natalie. If it matters to you, I can't sleep without the heaviest sleeping pills for the past eight years, dreaming of Deji and your son in my sleep. Dreaming of them pointing fingers at me."

That was the first time that Katherine told me about her demons. I had no idea she carried such guilt about that event. I sympathized with and even wanted to comfort her, knowing I too felt the same way many, many times over the years.

Hell, I thought, I may even drive all the way to her mansion and take her in my arms. Embracing Katherine with the similar pains I felt, offering her somewhat of a parallel feeling of understanding with my very being.

I thought more on this notion, and the weight of the past dawned on me like a suffocating beast, chaining my soul to agonies of what had transpired between Katherine and me before. Despite the new information and the new feelings of wanting to comfort her, I knew I could not bring myself to make the drive, let alone embrace Katherine – I feared we were more alike than I wanted to admit.

9

Two days later, I was back on a train again.

Not the route where my son and husband were kidnapped, but on another one to Liverpool. I'd booked first class and made sure the seat next to me wasn't taken. I was waiting for someone to join. The same someone I promised myself not to call earlier.

While waiting, I remembered one of my father's favorite insights into life. He hardly ever described anything as past or present. It was either truth or lies. To him, the only fact in life was the past. We've known it, experienced it, and though we occasionally would forget the details when, knew one thing about it: it really happened, thus the truth.

The future was simply lies.

Until the future happened and turned into the past, there was no telling how it turned out to be. So, whatever you expected of tomorrow was always going to remain lies until tomorrow when it was either confirmed or denied.

The present was the tricky part, one he didn't like to dabble with. Even for an artist like him, who understood how being present was the secret to creativity, he still called it a temporary lie or an attempt to make something true.

I run my brush on this palette and know what I want to do, but before it's done, before I paint my truth, hardly anything is what it seems, Snowflake. And it's part of our misery that we can only believe in the past. Because what if the past treated us poorly, and the future was to treat us better? We still have only one point of reference from what happened before. That's why people fail to believe in the future. It takes a great leap of faith to cross over and turn lies into truth.

"I'm sorry I'm late," Jason Ross said, sitting next to me, looking neat and handsome.

"No worries," I said. "I feel like we're hiding from something. Why did you want to meet here?"

"It's not ideally the best place to be, but I thought you and I taking a route we never took before was good enough," he said as the train took off.

"Good enough for what?"

"For answering the questions, you want me to," he said. "I didn't expect you to dig deep into my life, but when you sent me the message about your mother and Natalie, I realized I might be helpful to you."

I didn't quite understand what he said. It seemed like he was gaslighting, saying whole sentences that only added to my confusion. Finally, I said, "Does that mean that your answers will have nothing to do with the train incident?"

"Not really. Had they been, I'd have tamed the painful fire in my chest about my daughter and wife," he said, looking around, making sure he wasn't too loud, "I know things seem to be connected in the weirdest ways, but they never led me to know more about what happened that day. So, ask me. I promise I won't hold back. I like you enough to do that."

I didn't know what he meant by liking me, but I thought he seemed as if he was a tad more nervous than last time. I skipped the thought — or a slip of the tongue — and focused on why I was here: I didn't believe Katherine told me everything, and he was my only lead to further information.

"Well, let's start with my mother and Natalie. Did you know they worked together?"

"Sure. Katherine is the best psychologist in London. I hear she is a pain in the arse — sorry for bringing that up — but she is the best."

"Did you meet my mother in person?"

"No, Natalie wouldn't let that happen. We kept work rigidly separate from our private lives."

"Did you ever connect the dots and think it was odd my mother being Natalie's friend?"

"The truth is that I did, many times," Jason said, "It sounds like there must be a connection, but it also sounds like it can be just a vague, not quite connected, series of incidents. It's a small world. Ever heard about the six degrees of Kevin Bacon? It's a theory that we definitely will find one we know throughout every six people we come across."

I nodded in agreement. That's what I felt like as well. Emma's spiritual insight of there never being a coincidence rang through my head. I quickly pushed the thought away and attempted to change the direction of the conversation to find out what else he knew or could offer me.

"Did you know my husband?"

"No."

"Never met him?"

"I'm a businessman, Kate — you don't mind if I call you Kate, right? I take care of Welcome Homes' public relations. I hardly meet with immigrants."

"Could you explain that, please? What it is exactly that you do?"

"An organization like Welcome Home, though non-profit, is financed by donations from the rich," he said. "The rich don't quite know how to talk to the poor immigrants. They want to do good in the world, though, so they talk to guys who speak multiple languages and look good in tailored suits like me. Men and women who know how to dine and fluff talk the wealthy yet persuade them to donate to Welcome Home. If I hadn't met Natalie, I wouldn't have been concerned with the immigrants. I'm trying my best to be transparent here."

"I see," I considered. "But why do the rich donate or invest in Welcome Home in the first place — other than wanting to do good as you and my mother keep saying."

Jason pursed his lips while unbuttoning his suit, "Look, the reality is that the rich donate mostly to avoid taxes. That's not saying that some of them don't mean good. It's a complex world. There is also the fact that charity gatherings like these give room for the rich to communicate with their rich people, which leads to more business deals, social life, and occasionally marriage."

His words made sense. My impression of him being disconnected from the absolute misery in the world while ironically working for Welcome Home, which claims to be helping the miserable rang true. I wanted to ask more about Welcome Home but then reminded myself that the reason behind all of this was my son and husband.

"Can I ask you a personal question?" I tried to sound sympathetic, hoping he wouldn't see right through me.

"Shoot."

"I googled you and Natalie; you know that, right?"

"I don't blame you. You're a mother looking for answers. What about it?"

"I didn't find one picture of you and Natalie or Mila, your daughter, together," I said without asking the question itself. My interrogation was apparent enough.

Jason licked his lips and loosened his tie. He stopped looking at me and stared ahead into nothingness. It was as if he took a moment of silence to remember his family or something. He took his time, not caring to answer me. His demeanor changed. He seemed more human to me at that moment.

"Truth is," he said. "We kept our marriage secret. We didn't have to get married and could've kept the relationship secret, but I wanted her. I wanted to let her know how serious I was."

"So, no one knew until she died, huh. I suppose that's when documents and papers about your marriage surfaced?"

"You could say that."

"May I ask why you kept it secret?"

"Welcome Home Inc., Like I said earlier, rigid" he turned to face me.

"Okay?"

"You see, Natalie left the company at some point. We weren't in a relationship then. We only met later at a company party. And when that happened, Welcome Home wouldn't have approved of our relationship because of the lawsuit."

"Lawsuit?"

"Natalie discovered something unsavory about the company that she detested. She filed a lawsuit, and it was contained. When I say contained, I mean by higher powers. How, when, or why, I was never told. Even she made me promise her never to ask and consider it a forgotten past."

"Is your company involved in something shady?"

He laughed, "I'm telling you too much now. I didn't expect that. Did anyone tell you that you have that something that makes people tell you things?"

"Not really. I don't talk to many strangers. I'm an introvert."

"Oh," he said.

"Oh, what?"

"I didn't realize you still thought of me as a stranger," he said, grinning. "Anyway, Natalie and I got married. I loved her. I'm only saying it in past tense because she is probably gone by now, or whatever that means."

I liked the way he talked about her with such fondness. I liked that his moist eyes couldn't hide his affection for someone he obviously loved.

"So, Mila isn't your daughter?"

"No. She is the daughter of the Russian police officer who raped Natalie years ago back home," he says with disdain.

"I'm sorry," I didn't know what to say, again realizing how much I didn't consider people's pain in the past and only focused on myself being a victim. There was something cathartic about meeting someone with whom you shared a painful connection. "I guess I should stop asking so many questions. I'm sorry."

"No, go ahead and ask me," he reached for his pocket and pulled out eye drops. "I'll just use these for a second. I'm sorry. I used to wear contact lenses. That's why I need the drops from time to time. London and all the pollution hurts my eyes, you know."

"I understand," I said, watching a man I thought had the world at the tip of his hands nearly breakdown before my eyes. I almost felt guilty doing this to him with my pestering and longing for information.

"So, you don't know what Welcome Home did to Natalie?"

"We call it the W, short for the long name. It's how investors call it. The W as in *welcome* and *win*," he tucked the drops into his pocket but kept his head craned upward. "To answer your question, no. Natalie wouldn't tell me, and I frankly never asked because it's a good-paying job. I wouldn't know what to do for a living had I left."

"But you don't think they didn't know about your relationship. How much could you hide from such a big firm?"

"Natalie thought so too. The bottom line was probably not to make it public and hurt the W's reputation. I wasn't sure. It happened fast, and I was in love. It felt good and challenging. We never met in private while in London. It was all weekend in Mykonos, Tuscany, and so on. What I loved the most was Mila liking me. It was a new experience that I cherished a lot."

"I want to ask you this one last time but don't get mad at me," I said. "You think that all of this has nothing to do with the W or my mother?"

"I wouldn't lie to you. It doesn't. I see that you seem to lean into something fishy having gone wrong that day," he lowered his head and blinked. "I never thought of it like that. I keep thinking that the investigation didn't care about the victims as much as the overall propaganda about a terrorist attack. Had this been a simple robbery, I think our loved ones would have been given better attention."

"I want to believe what you said is true, but I still doubt the absence of something fishy."

"I understand. I'm glad I met you, though," he said, smiling a little. "I mean, this conversation alone feels so good. Thank you."

I liked the way he stared at me, but hell no. Even though I let my mind wander before, I decided I could no longer indulge the romantic so-called 'feelings' or whatever you wanted to call it that were sparking between us. All these romantically tinged thoughts were red alerts to me, sirens sounding off from the tops of the walls built around my heart. Even last time, I felt too comfortable around him.

Stay strong, Snowflake. Getting romantically involved with him would not be ideal. Besides, you're not in a romantic comedy.

"My mother wondered if the terrorists were ever immigrants she'd recommended to stay in her reports," I changed the mood with my inquisitive words.

"Okay?" He responded with a slight disappointment because I wouldn't let him charm me with his stare.

"Do you think that is possible? Did the police tell you anything about the terrorists other than that they wanted to exchange the hostages for prisoners in the UK? Did the W maybe know something about the terrorists?"

"The W never gave the incident much thought. We have so many immigrants we want to help. I was never told the terrorists were immigrants...."

Suddenly a woman nearby screamed, the piercing sound breaking our focus, interrupting our thoughts.

I craned my head to look over the seats while she claimed someone had stolen her purse. This being London, no one did anything but stare. The best they did was film the incident with their phones. It was a sudden and strange incident that felt like a pebble to the head after being so immersed in the conversation with Jason. I turned back to say something clever, despite the red flags and sirens going on within.

He was gone.

I stood up and ran to the door. The train had stopped, and when I peeked out, I saw him running after the thief who had taken the woman's purse. I couldn't believe this was real before my eyes. If my father's voice in my head thought that falling for him in any way was out of a romantic comedy, what was I supposed to call this?

A few minutes later, Jason came back with the woman's purse. She oddly thanked him with a kiss on the cheek. Even she couldn't resist him, I supposed.

When I asked him why he let the thief go, he said he was a poor immigrant, and Jason didn't feel like being the one ruining his life.

Hearing how honorable he acted was nearly too much for me. I was looking for answers to the mystery that shrouded my life, not liking someone too much for my own good.

"Listen," I said, pulling my hair behind my ears. "I have to go, but thanks for everything."

"But wait," he said, suddenly waving a pound note at me, "I have enough money to ask you out for dinner."

I couldn't suppress a smile. It would reform into a genuine laugh, but I couldn't allow myself to do it.

"Are you flashing your money at me?" I said with furrowed brows.

"The old woman rewarded me with a pound and said I'd better ask you out before I grow old and someone steals my bag," he smirked in a boyish way that reminded me of Deji's flirtations.

"I can't. I'm sorry," I said, feigning disappointment. Like always, my body language betrayed me somehow, and his keen, interrogating eyes saw it.

"The Rosemary Diner, 9 pm this weekend?" He titled his head, staring into my soul. "Life is short, and whether we like it or not, another train is coming for us sooner or later."

10

"You're dating him?" Emma said with eyes wide open. "What the fuck, Kate?"

"I know," I said, embarrassed while cooking in my kitchen. Emma had just finished teaching yoga to her clients and then passed by to hear all about my love life in detail. "I'm not supposed to, but I do."

"Not supposed to?" She nudged me. "You see how good-looking this S.O.B. is?"

"You don't mind?" Jason's good looks and money hadn't been part of my equation. Both were a bonus for sure, but nothing compared to how he made me feel safe, comfortable, and secure.

"Does he have a brother?" She nudged me again. "Tell me he has a twin, please."

"You're dating every fit athlete in London, Emma. Please let me have this one," I winked back at her, which I was terrible at. In all the years of our friendship, I tried to mirror her flirtatiousness and sassiness but failed miserably.

"My boys don't dress that good," she rolled her eyes. "They look good topless but not in suits, but this bad boy here, whew," she pointed at his picture on social media. "He is a Daniel Craig James Bond. Is he good in bed?"

"Seriously?" I took a step away from her and groaned. "Do people ask stuff like that?"

She moved closer, teasing me, "I need to know. Tell me."

"I'm not telling you. Get away from me. Go pick the seasoning for the pasta on the top shelf, nasty friend."

"Nasty best friend," she corrected me while picking up the seasoning Deji taught me to use. Najimbian delicious flavors.

"Not for long," I warned her. "I'm not telling you about my sex life. Why would you even want to know that?"

"I'll tell you about mine."

"You tell me about *them* all the time. Each boy is a new flavor of the month to you. It's much more personal to me, not like yours in the slightest."

"Okay, Mother Teresa," she handed me the seasoning. "I just wondered how it felt having sex after being celibate for eight years."

Her words almost made me stop stirring the sauce. Never once had I thought of myself as a celibate in those years. I was busy, I guessed. Letting her words sink in, I realized that it wasn't being busy. I had just dismissed the idea of getting intimate with anyone again.

"Well, I guess it means he is also good," she said. "I told you that you're lucky with men. A hot, rich, and good-in-bed-hunk — in your thirties, chapeau girl, I love you," she held my head with her hands and kissed my cheeks. "Don't let this one go."

"Even though you're a little too touchy, I appreciate it," I teased her. "Really. I thought it didn't make sense to date the man who lost his family on the same train. I can't tell you how guilty I feel about it sometimes."

"It's a train, Kate," she glared at me. "It's almost impossible to date someone in the same city who hadn't been on the same train once. Trains are condoms, the lubricator of crossroads, it gets you there, but the machine itself is of no importance. It's the destination," she motioned a finger at her head, pointing out how crazy she sounded, then looked at the half-full bottle of wine next to her. "Okay. I'm officially drunk."

"I can see that," I said but then returned to the matter at hand, "Jason's family died on the same train my family died. It's different."

"You're not a Snowflake, snowflake," she whispered in my ears. "Everybody fucks everybody. Everybody wants everybody. Life is not a game of chess where you plan and execute. It's a Roulette. Roll the dice and grab your slice."

"I wish I was you, really," I nudged her away to shove the pasta bowl into the oven. "You make it sound simple."

"It's simple. It's all meaningless. We're here. We're gone. Let's have some fun," she began dancing to the rhythm of her own beat with the wine bottle in her hand. "You should call DCI Tom Holmes tomorrow, by the way."

"Wait. What did you say?"

"He was trying to reach you, but you've changed your number," she said casually. "He asked for it, but you told me not to give it away, so I said I'd take a message."

"Did he say what it was about?" I tried to hide the desperation behind the question.

"He wants you to meet him at the station tomorrow. He said something about you having to fill out formal papers or something."

I shrugged, attempting to brush it off. I hadn't seen DCI Tom Holmes in years and tried to reign in my already wandering thoughts about why he could possibly want to see me after all this time. He was the one responsible for Deji's and Andrew's case.

11

Dating Jason was an unusual experience for me. I mean, I had only been with two men before Deji, and after eight years of unintentional celibacy, it felt surreal. Foolishly enough, in my younger days, I used to think that each boy I was with would be the boy I'd live with for the rest of my life. Katherine had always commented that I may have inherited it from my father. Believe it or not, Kyle Mason told me he'd only been with Katherine — which I doubted, as he was a charmer.

Kyle and I always stood out as either liars or utterly dreamy and stupid when it came to our not so adventurous sex lives. Especially me. None of the people I've met in my life had so few partners, especially in their younger years. I've always wanted someone to create something with.

Love-making seemed to be a means for something more significant in my mind, though Katherine said it was all about the art. She called my father and me egotistical artists who only cared about their creativity and wanted someone to cuddle with when they were tired of spending hours in our solitary state of mental masturbation.

Colorful masturbation on my palette, I love it. My father used to tease her, *don't tell me I didn't put blood and sweat into those paintings.*

Then I met Deji while he was my mother's personal trainer. She didn't need him for toning her body and chronic back pain, but rather to show him off to everyone — sort of disguised slavery in the current century and the fact that she could tote around a sexy man in front of all her friends.

Deji was shy. He had a sense of acceptance in his soul I hadn't experienced before. Him being an immigrant, escaping blood-shed lands, and given the opportunity to make a decent living and being treated like a human being meant the world to him. He wasn't here to date, make lots of money, or have higher aspirations. He was content and grateful — and he sent money back home, even after our marriage, to someone I dared not ask about. Later I learned he didn't send it back home, but somewhere here in Britain.

Being as shy and introverted as I was, it took me months to ask him out. Even though the physical and emotional attraction was instant, I knew he'd never risk his job. Silly enough, we bonded over prank videos on YouTube. It was the only reason we could steal moments, sitting side by side, thighs to thighs and shoulder to shoulder, enjoying the company as we pointed at the videos on our phones. Almost as if we were a couple of pre-teens awkwardly sharing a moment of insecure laughter, longing for so much more.

This went on for quite some time until I sent him a text asking if *he'd want to have a bite late tonight.*

"Only if you start texting in proper English," he teased me on the phone. "Wanna, gonna, dunno, ha?"

I let him have a bite of me that night and me of him. We couldn't resist each other. Not that it was in my nature, but the tension that had been building between us was too strong to ignore any further.

There was so much pressure on him afterward, and he wanted to stop seeing me. He hadn't started his own fitness YouTube channel then, and Katherine — and her obnoxious friends — were his only source of income. Despite the gawking and drooling over him, they all paid him handsomely.

It took me several more months to persuade him to leave the job and start his own company. He was reluctant. I could tell Katherine had this power over him, which I never fully understood. The first time he told her he wanted to leave the job and start his own company, she refused and started the idea of therapy.

"You're doing what with my mother?" I remember asking him in a fit of anger.

"It's good for me," he explained. "Katherine is a good listener, and she has good advice. She helps me with my past back in NajimbiNajimbiaa."

"You can tell me about your past. I'm here for you."

"You wouldn't understand," he said. "As my partner, I don't want you to know what happened to me. You will not understand."

"I will, Deji," I calmed myself down and apologized for my recklessness. "I'll do anything for you, and I will never judge you."

That night he held me by the shoulders and let his eyes stare into mine. His grip was stronger than usual, yet a little jittery, "I don't want to tell anyone about it."

"But you tell Katherine."

"Because she makes it as if I'm talking to a wall. I can't explain it, but she does, and it helps. I trust her not ever to tell anyone. I trust her to never tell herself. She has magic. I can't explain. It's good for me."

That was the first time I realized he believed in superstitions. *She has magic. I can't explain it. So, couldn't I explain it? I was simply introduced to the first rule about relationships: you get to accept things you couldn't understand about one another, or it wouldn't work out.*

"Great show, right?" Jason told me, bringing me back to real life, away from my inner thoughts. We left the theatre, watching a Russian play Natalie and her daughter liked. It was about revolutions and not giving up. I hardly understood much of it. Neither did he, as his Russian wasn't that good. I had difficulty reading translations while watching the mesmerizing ballet sketches and incredible singing. But as Jason told me earlier, I left the theatre feeling high and full of hope.

"I didn't expect it to touch me like this without understanding what they were saying," I said, engaging his arm and resting my hand over his shoulder.

"That's what art is. It can't be described but felt," he sighed, walking with me into the lobby. "You have the same thing about you."

"What do you mean?" I rubbed his arm, feeling uncannily safe and sound around him.

"There is something about you that makes me want to stay," he said. "I'd argue it's your charm, looks, voice, touch, or whatever we like to pinpoint to give reason to our unreasonable feelings. I don't understand a bloody thing when you draw, but I love it."

"You don't like my paintings, admit it," I chuckled.

"Rationally, no, but irrationally I'm all in."

He opened the door to his Mercedes for me, and I got in. I was in a haze as he drove in silence. The city lights late at night seemed like magic lanterns swaying on both our sides. The contrast between the blackness of night and everything glowing in gold around us took my breath away. I knew that I was over enjoying everything around me. I mean, London hardly drapes its romantic vibes on its pedestrians. It's not Paris by any stretch of the imagination.

I felt his words echoing in my mind. *But irrationally, I'm all in.*

Oh, boy, how I felt that. There was nothing rational about us dating. He did his best to make more of a friendship where we enjoyed our times. We never went to restaurants or did that candle-lit dinner thing. It was always a surprise – the opera, movies, skating, silly youngster activities, and even surprised me with tickets to art galleries I couldn't even enjoy with Deji.

He never asked me about the future. We never talked about the past. It was an unspoken rule between us – to be fully and wholly present. The only places we avoided and wouldn't talk about passing by were train stations, trains, and anything that reminded us of those we had lost.

I began taking Uber instead of trains since I met him. Too expensive for me, but it was a cost I paid in the steps I had taken to move on. I did it reluctantly, with a twitch in my heart every time I blamed myself for allowing myself to move on despite my initial strength and determination.

Did you give up on them, Kate? Kyle Mason would remind me of my best moments with Jason. *Did you give up on Deji and Andrew?*

"Want to grab a drink at my house?" Jason said while driving.

I was looking outside my window when he asked. Without looking back, I said, "You know I'm not ready yet."

"I understand."

"I'm really sorry...."

"Don't mention it," he said, reaching for my hand and squeezing it. "I shouldn't be pushing it.

Fuck, he was so good to me. So much that I sometimes resented it.

"You know Emma thinks we've been having sex all the time?" I turned to face him with a smile.

"Oh," he chuckled. "I can't blame her. I don't know many men who have superpowers to hold themselves back from you."

"Shut up," I laughed, blushing at the comment. "She said that about you. She said you were hot like James Bond."

"Whoa," he took a left. "James Bond is a lover of women. I just loved one, "he stopped himself mid-sentence, catching us both off guard.

None of the others uttered the word 'love' before. Was that love? Though we hadn't spoken about it, I never thought of it as love. Deji was love. It felt different. It felt unstoppable and star-crossed. We were two people who helped one other overcome an inevitable pain that only both of us understood. A pain that words couldn't describe but better expressed in silent and calmly reserved mornings.

"I'll drive you home," Jason changed the subject. "I have a lot of work tomorrow, and you my lady, are a beautiful distraction I can't resist."

As we passed by the police station, my smile was feeble, "Oh, I forgot."

"What?"

"Can you drive me back to the police station? I'm supposed to meet up with DCI Tom Holmes."

"The detective from the train incident?"

"He asked to meet me, and *you*, Sir, were a distraction all week. Just drop me off. Don't wait for me. I'll take an Uber back."

"If you say so," he said, turning back without asking too many questions.

I liked this about Jason. It's been two months of dating, and he wanted things to go smooth.

At the station, I got off and closed the door behind me. I looked back inside the car and spoke. "Maybe we should slow down with seeing each other?"

Again, his eyes looked back in shock, but he seemed collected. He nodded without saying the words. I guess he couldn't bring himself to say it.

"It's not that I don't think it's working," I said. "It's actually because I think I like you too much."

12

DCI Tom Holmes was in his mid-fifties. He looked the part of the classic worn-out and tired detective like in the movies. His most common features were grey and receding hair and a goatee over a slight tan. He always wore glasses but took them off whenever he interacted with someone or read something. He was silent and deliberately slow as if every movement had an intention and purpose. His eyes never betrayed his true feelings. He just pierced through you with solid intensity. Part of his job, it seemed, was to say little and show fewer emotions. I knew him long enough, and as much as I berated and insulted him for not solving the crime, he never responded or took it to heart.

There was nothing to love or hate about him. No matter how much time I spent talking to him, it felt like talking to a voice on a hotline service of some company: all information and facts without emotion or logical reasoning. I'd assumed it came with the territory of his job and not a personality flaw. It suited him perfectly anyway.

"Tom," I shook his hand. We were over formalities after all these years.

"Nice to see you, Kate," he said over the desk and showed me where to sit. "You changed your phone number."

"I'm not a wanted fugitive, am I?" I countered back. "I can do that, right?"

"Technically, yes, but it was hard to find you," he took off his glasses and read a document before him. "So let me be brief about this."

"Please be."

"It's been eight years," he raised his stern eyes at me.

I nodded silently, anticipating.

"Emma said you decided to move on."

"She can't stop telling, huh. Does that bother you?"

"Not the least. I'm just a man working to make ends meet. If you ask me, you should've moved on last year."

"Pardon me?"

"Are you aware that your husband and son aren't considered missing?"

"Deji and Andrew," I had to utter their names. The police like to treat victims in stereotypes. "I'm not sure what you're saying."

"After seven years of missing persons, they're automatically declared dead by the law," he said bluntly, his tone and voice matching the lack of emotion in his eyes.

"They are?" I uttered in almost disbelief. I realized I never even thought about it.

"It's the law."

"They'll always be missing to me."

"And I'll always pretend that I love my job though it gives me headaches, and no one ever appreciates what I do," he said without emotion. I couldn't tell whether he was stoically joking or just spitting facts.

"Tom," I said firmly. "What do you want from me?"

He pushed the document toward me, "Sign it."

My eyes briefly ran over it. I was about to sign a release form declaring my husband and son dead.

"What if I don't want to?"

"Then the government will sign it on your behalf," he said. "I'm only saving you the hassle of hiring lawyers and having to do so much paperwork, including the death certificates and process that has to do with whether you and your now-deceased husband owned the apartment or whether it now becomes yours, etc."

"I'm not signing it. They've waited a year, Tom. They can wait for more."

"They've waited a year because I asked them to. Whatever cold bastard you think I am, I respect you and what you've been through, so I delayed it until I found you. I understand you don't want to sign because of the sentiment that they're still coming back, but to the government, they're officially gone. You can't even re-open the case anymore."

Silence draped all over my existence. Was this it? Did I unconsciously know that the missing was declared dead after seven years, so I decided to wait one more year to move on?

"So you're telling me nothing new happened in the case?" I had to ask.

"Nothing new will happen, Kate. You know how many other terrorist attacks we have had in London since then?"

"Thirteen," I said.

"You did your research, but do you know how many were solved or have definite answers?"

"None," I nearly whispered as I swallowed my pain in the form of my tasteless saliva.

"Good," he said. "Sign it then."

"Did Jason Ross sign it?" The question popped in my head, and my mouth ran away with the thought before I could even think twice.

Tom grimaced. It was as if he wondered why I specifically asked about him.

"He is a reasonable man," Tom said. "He will sign it."

"He will?" I tilted my head. "So he didn't?"

Tom pursed his lips and shook his head ever so slightly, "He didn't."

"Why?"

"I take it back about him being a reasonable man. He is a stubborn bastard like...."

"Like me," I said. "What did he say exactly?"

"He said his wife and daughter — who isn't even his daughter by birth— might still be out there somewhere, and nothing proves they're dead."

I smiled, proud of Jason. "I'm surprised you remember," I stood up. "Please let the government kiss...."

"Don't say what he said, please."

"What did Jason say?"

"Let's say he cursed in words that break all expected etiquette of a rich man like him."

"I'm not going to curse, Tom," I shook his hand. "I'm just not going to give up on a case the government barely cared about."

I left the station and ordered an Uber while a strange euphoric feeling ran through my body. I was at peace with myself. Had they asked me to sign this paper years ago, I'd have felt even better denying them the pleasure.

Something about formally declaring to the police that I'd never stop looking for Deji and Andrew healed a part of me. It made me understand that I wasn't giving up by moving on. I only decided to enjoy the gift of life I was given. It didn't mean I wouldn't keep looking to know what happened or find my family if they were alive. It just meant that dying while alive wasn't going to help me find them. I needed to nourish my soul and strengthen it by not giving into darkness and shrinking into the oblivion of hopelessness.

I was so proud of Jason as I was of myself.

So proud that I canceled the Uber, knowing Jason would come back for me instantly. I felt so alive, more than I had felt in years, so reckless and drunk on life from the sudden epiphany that I had reached. I felt overjoyed and did not want to waste another minute feeling anything other than bliss and love for the time was truly now; everything had aligned itself to be so. I called Jason, and he picked up on the first ring.

"Hello?"

"Jason, I have two questions for you."

"Ok, shoot"

"Would you please come back to the police station to pick me up?"

"Sure, I kept cruising around, hoping you'd call. What's the next question?"

"Would you do me the honor and make me the happiest woman on Earth and marry me?"

13

EIGHT YEARS AGO…

When Andrew was six years old, Deji bought him a Fisher-Price train set. I'd heard them returning home on a Sunday while still working on one of my father's paintings, trying to see if a few touches would increase its price on eBay. It was a brightly colored oil painting of me as a child. While it did have sentimental value, portraits of anonymous children were trending on eBay then. I never sold it — and its other similar copies at Katherine's mansion because I looked too cute in my dad's eyes. That wasn't me at all.

The unmatched state of mirth Andrew was in urged me to stop my work and leave the room to check on them. I stood over them, kneeling on the ground, playing with this clunky and rubbery toy train. It was as brightly colored as my painting, vibrant and loud. Over time this train would become Andrew's favorite toy, and he gradually wore its color off due to so many sessions of playtime.

He crawled on the floor, pulling the long string of locomotives across the room, not allowing anyone to touch it without permission. This train was so precious to him - a gift from his father, his idol and a favorite thing at that, a train. It was almost too unique.

Whenever I cleaned the house, I couldn't move it from its latest location. In Andrew's logic, it wasn't because he was going to throw a fit of tears at me, but because of a pretty convincing reason — at least in his mind. *No one moved the train but its driver, w*hich was Andrew, of course!

Andrew had found a toy conductor that fit perfectly in the front of the train. Of course, this toy was a batman figurine, and he drove the train. Deji and I laughed at the logic, but even more that we had no say in debating it. Deji would sometimes tear up in laughter with all things concerning the train. One night he spent two hours explaining why Andrew's childhood happiness brought him to tears. In Deji's childhood, he'd never known that a child could be that happy and excited instead of running away from the fear hunting him.

Ouna. Ouna.

The day Deji bought the train, I had to question the reason gently. It was a bit too expensive, purchased from a luxury toy shop we never even glanced at because we knew the costs of their toys. I found the timing a bit straining, especially when Deji needed surgery for a muscle hernia from too much training — he had to keep up with his image for his business to flourish. Deji explained that he had no choice, pointing at the train's front, a smiley face with a slightly darker complexion. I had to admit the train was perfect for our perfect boy and let the worry of money wash away when I saw the pure happiness in both of my boy's eyes.

That wasn't why Andrew insisted on having it. While Deji was looking to buy a present for one of his client's kids, Andrew eyed the train from the shop window as they were walking past. Some sneaky and intelligent marketer had printed names on the train's faces. This train was called Andrew.

Since then, this has been my son's favorite fixation, and I learned it was the same for many others. I learned that we should've bought him a smaller train as a toddler as they fascinated him. Something about trains made him go crazy, but the train with the same name as his, well, it was his most prized possession.

Deji once told me that he read in a study that trains were one of the easiest ways to form a bond with a child. It was an easy toy to

move, safe for a child, and the fact that everyone played with them —
and paid their respects in the case of Andrew — made it a feasible
bringer of joy for all. So the Runaway Train, that was what we were
instructed by Andrew to call it, brought joy, killed time while I was
busy doing things to run the household or when creative drive called
to me, and even put him to sleep occasionally for his afternoon naps.

It even helped with his education. Be it a train on TV, in a magazine, or real life, he began to love them and learn about them. He
began to ask Deji how they moved and why they weren't as fast as
motorcycles and planes. Deji smartly inserted all kinds of educa-
tional ideas into the subject, from gravity or physics to even people's
safety and how trains allowed people to communicate.

Then and there, I should've known Deji was just as fascinated
with the train. How could I have suspected that Deji was the one who
suggested they call it the Runaway Train?

14

It turned out that Katherine told Deji about the train study, which showcased parents bonding with their kids. Deji didn't want to mention it so I wouldn't get mad or feel that she was slyly sneaking in her influence on Andrew's upbringing. I'd made clear that Katherine wasn't allowed to interfere with raising my son. After all, she wanted only to bring him back to the mansion and raise him as a rich and spoiled grandson, selfishly keeping him all to herself.

What bothered me was not understanding her intentions in telling Deji about the study. I mean, and I was aware of my insecurity due to the very nature of the relationship between my husband and my son. I felt Deji and Andrew connected more over the train than Andrew and I. In a way, I felt outcasted.

You're not insecure, Snowflake. My father's imaginary voice told me. *You're only afraid that the way you grew attached to me and hating your mother would oppositely happen with Andrew. You think it's Karma.*

Sometimes before sleep, I needed to tell myself affirmations about my childhood. I needed to remind myself that I didn't do anything wrong to Katherine. She was the one who repeatedly admitted she didn't like the way I grew up detesting the rich life.

A few weeks later, Katherine called me to tell me that Andrew seemed above average in his intelligence than what other children his age was averaging. She suggested I'd check his IQ to see if she was correct in her suspicions.

Stay away from my son, Katherine. Don't attempt to change him into what you want him to be like you did to me. Let him enjoy being a child.

Still, my insecurity drove me to find a way to connect with Andrew over the train, as much as Deji did.

That was when the Choo Choo song came into our lives.

Cha cha cha cha, choo choo train,
Rolling down the choo choo lane,
I hear your whistle blowing loud (choo choo)
1, 2, 3, 4, 5, 6, 7, 8
9, 10, 11, 12
13, 14, 15, 16
17, 18, 19, 20
Here we go!

The song saved me from secretly envying Deji and Andrew's bonding. Previously when they played with the train for so long on the floor, I had no place to sit next to them, so I was left on the outskirts of the intimate playtime. Deji was a huge man, and the living room was relatively small unless we moved couches. So, when I figured out how to sneak myself in between them, I didn't know how to play along. There was not enough room, but I was also lost in what the intricate storylines were, unable to capture the narrative between them and the train.

The imaginary story they had built of the Runaway Train was too deep, and they couldn't follow up. I resigned myself to the fact that this feeling of being left out kept me worried — and I knew that I shouldn't have. Yet as his mother, I couldn't help but feel benevolent jealousy forming inside me, no matter how I tried to avoid it.

The weeks when the Runaway Train came into our lives were when Deji and I decided we weren't going to have any more kids. It was apparent that we couldn't handle it financially for a few years, and by then, we decided we would be too old.

So, to tamp down my jealously, I researched children and trains. I came to find out how almost none of them rejected the Choo Choo song. Something about the phonetics of the words made children love it. Deji had never heard of the song and didn't have an equivalent in his Najimbian language, so Andrew welcomed my invention with open arms.

Finally, I found my place in his child's play. Deji helped in conducting the train. I was the soundtrack that gave it strength and made its main conductor, Andrew Olanti, happy. Fair game.

Despite his happy, go-lucky nature, Andrew was different than other kids. Maybe remarkable, like Katherine said. One day he returned with a decision: the Choo Choo songs needed to change.

The first rule was that the number's part had to be a countdown because he saw them do it this way on YouTube with racing cars. A countdown indicated that something was about to happen. Of course, he never expressed it in these words, but when I understood, I only realized what it meant in actuality a few years later.

Also, the countdown had to be from 10 downward because a 20 countdown was too long for him. He was the conductor, and it was Andrew's Train, so he changed it to:

Cha cha cha cha, choo choo train,
Rolling down the choo choo lane,
I hear your whistle blowing loud (choo choo)
10, 9, 8, 7, 6,
5, 4, 3, 2, 1
Mum N Pa go!

The last part was the second rule. We had to abide by it. Deji and I were all too happy to be fully enthralled in his game. We had to 'go' whenever he said 'go,' and we loved every minute of it.

I'd already shoved the train under his bed later. So, I was glad I didn't stumble over it when I emptied the box of documents earlier. That toy train would eventually show up in the pictures, so I also shoved all the photos under the bed, avoiding my good memories in life like a plague.

Why the fuck did you not take the car that day, Deji?

15

THREE MONTHS AGO...

Jason looked like James Bond in his wedding suit. So much that not one woman of the attendees took her eyes off him. Admittedly, they weren't many, but most of them weren't from my side of the family. Only Emma and Katherine — and her two obnoxious besties — were mine.

Strangely enough, Jason's family was the quietest and most welcoming, though also the most distant. He'd explained to me earlier that they wished him the best but didn't want to interfere in his life. He vaguely hinted at them objecting to his job at the W, and I didn't quite understand why.

Emma brought a fiancé that day, much to my own surprise. She was not one I would have expected to ever settle down. He was a good-looking man who oddly was also in his forties. I somehow knew she had tricked him. She wasn't going to marry him anyway, but she didn't want to attend the wedding either single or with a 'boyfriend.' It had to be a fiancé to match the occasion. She once told me that women who didn't marry had to live up to society's scrutiny and play games the older they got.

It didn't bother me. She was my best friend. If I experienced jealousy as a mother, I'd forgive her for not knowing how to balance what she wanted out of men. She was right when she said I was lucky with men. On the other hand, the almost sixty-year-old Katherine did flirt around on in the wedding. I'd heard stories by then, and I knew her tendencies. However, her strongest trait was discretion — and understanding of who society needed her to be at any given moment.

I'd offer you lots of gifts for your wedding, even a better house, but I know you'd let me down, she had said when I sent her the invitation. *Did you marry a rich man to get rid of needing me, once and for all?*

I hung up the phone that day, disgusted by her comments. She was also upset that I suddenly told her I was getting married. I'd never even hinted at dating someone earlier. Neither did Jason. He was good at keeping a low key about wives and girlfriends, which was a slightly worrying attribute.

"I'm afraid he'd done that before," Emma told me once. "I hope he won't ask you for a secret wedding like Natalie. I mean, he's hot and gentle, but men are men."

Jason didn't. He couldn't help but tell everyone. I thought I'd never seen a happier man about him getting married like that. Not even Deji.

I stood in my white — and otherworldly expensive — tailored dress, looking in the mirror, ready to leave the room and go outside to attend the ceremony. Jason was Catholic, and I pretended I was too, so we brought in a priest and avoided another ceremony in a church. When I say 'pretend,' I meant that I'd lost my faith in higher powers years ago. Since Kyle and Katherine were of the Catholic faith, and I met Jason, I contemplated whether it mattered.

Deji, a Muslim, didn't practice his religion as well. He had this idea that the human part of religion, meaning those in authority, wasn't to be trusted. As for the spiritual vision, he was all in. The solution? He always said, "I believe in the one powerful and unseen unknown that created this beautiful world. Whoever you are, and whatever reasons kept you from announcing yourself clearly without a doubt, I know you care for me and so I will do my best to be the best of who I can be."

Standing in the room now and staring at the mirror, I fought the tears welling in my eyes. I wanted to mouth the words, 'I love you, Deji,' but thought it was unfair to Jason.

"I love you, Andrew, and I'll trade my life for yours anytime," I said to the mirror. It was fair to everyone.

Emma, the hairdresser, and the tailor had done their job already with their latest touches and gave me a moment to catch my breath alone in the room.

"Don't you dare change your mind," Emma hissed in my ears and spanked me on my behind on her way out, "or I'll have him on your behalf."

It was ironic knowing that she couldn't have him. I reckoned that no other women at this time could have had Jason. It didn't matter how much he said he liked me, and I still thought he was attracted to me because of our common trauma. I didn't dislike it. I was reading too much Paulo Coelho at the time. His stories usually had people bonding over trauma. To him, trauma and pain were their own beauty and beast. And though these were cliched words that I hardly understood, Jason helped me give in to them. I wasn't getting married today out of a desperate need for intimacy. Neither was it lust or money. Neither was it safety. I was literally moving on. Finally.

Life wasn't going to stop, and I was going to get old. Deji and Andrew will forever have my heart. Jason was going to get whatever they permitted him to have of it, knowing that I missed them so much.

I reminded myself that Jason was waiting.

He had rented this small townhouse for the wedding. We had agreed on living in my apartment for a while. I appreciated that, though he said he could only do it for three months, we had to find a new place for both of us. He promised to help me create a special room for my paintings and never bother me when I was inside. He told me that he understood how cathartic it was to me at this time in my life.

This man. Where did he come from? Why was he so good to me?

He joked about imagining we were both virgins and having sex on our wedding night. It was a lame joke, but I was the one to blame. He went on to tell me that he was okay with postponing sex while we were married until I felt okay with it. That part made me laugh. I had him in my dreams, making love to me for weeks already. I lusted after him so much that he had no idea.

My issue with the living situation was that I never felt connected to rich people's lives, so I didn't want to move to his condo on that expensive high-rise in London. At least not now.

I was ready.

I was ready to feel alive again.

I was ready to dream of a better tomorrow.

Just then, my phone beeped, pulling me instantly back down to Earth. I had left it in my purse by the bed as I had no intentions of taking any calls in the next hour. Also, almost everyone who'd typically called was waiting outside for me. Were they so impatient they had to urge me to walk down the aisle? Well, I was on my way out anyway, and there was no need to panic or check out the message. I smoothed my dress and took a deep breath, ready to step into my new life.

On my way to the door, it beeped again. Still, I wasn't going to pick up. Now was not the time.

Then it went on a frenzy of beeps—message after message after message. I couldn't believe this was happening. I decided I would just turn it on silent so I could focus on the bright future just ahead of me, right outside that door. Hesitantly, I returned and picked up my purse. Something deep in my core told me this wouldn't end up well. This wasn't a prank. I could feel it. I checked the messages, and they were from an unknown number: thirteen messages so far and counting.

I clicked it open and read it:

Cha cha cha cha, choo choo train,
Rolling down the choo choo lane,
I hear your whistle blowing loud (choo choo)

10, 9, 8, 7, 6,
5, 4, 3, 2, 1
Mum and Pa go!

16

Unlike the day I lost Deji and Andrew, I found myself alert and somehow calm. Part of me told me this wasn't possible. Part of me learned the lesson eight years ago: *don't fuckin' panic, Kate.*

The first thing I did was scroll through the messages, checking if there was more to read, but it was the same message repeatedly. They kept coming after I'd read them. Immediately, I called back the number, tapping my foot and convincing myself that my heartbeat wasn't drumming in my ears.

No answer.

I waited until it stopped, and then I dialed again. The messages stopped, but still, no one answered me.

Who are you? I messaged back.

Somehow, I knew I'd get no reply. I hurried to the door and ran outside. I had to tell Jason. Emma, maybe. I wasn't sure. But I had to tell someone. Almost stumbling my way out in the corridor, I reached the arch of flowers that led to the garden. Everyone looked at me with broad smiles and cheers. I guess they hadn't registered the panic on my face yet.

I realized I couldn't speak, still trying to call back the messenger.

All I did was put the phone on speaker and raise it in the air. Tears suddenly filled my eyes.

"Kate," Jason ran toward me. "What's wrong?"

My mouth was open, but the tears shook me, and I still couldn't speak. Jason glanced at the phone and then back to me but didn't understand.

"Does she need a doctor?" Katherine yelled with a wine glass in her hands. She was worried but also confused. "Talk to me, Kate."

Jason snatched the phone from my hand and looked again. He was trying to know who I was calling to get answers. It all happened fast, and I felt that I would panic myself to my grave eventually. The crowd suddenly realized what was going on and finally shut up. The clinking of glasses, the chatter, and the background music suddenly stopped. I hardly knew who was saying what, and the tears in my eyes almost blurred my vision.

In the silencing of the crowd, I heard something. It was the ring of a phone.

Everyone kept asking me what was going on, and I screamed at them, "Shut the fuck up!" Now that put them to grave silence. A terrible silence. Even the phone had stopped ringing. My eyes darted all around, then I snatched back the phone and redialed.

No one uttered a word. Their eyes were on me. The unknown phone rang again.

I ran like a maniac, following the sound. I think Jason did, too, even though he didn't understand why.

I tapped people's bodies in case one of them hid the phone. Pushed them around and made them stand up from their chairs. I didn't care for any one's feelings, accusing everyone of everything. Strange enough, I found the phone faster than I expected.

I found a cheap phone on the table, near Katherine, with the creepiest ringtone.

Cha cha cha cha, choo choo train, Rolling down the choo choo lane, I hear your whistle blowing loud (choo choo)

Never had kids singing given me such goosebumps before.

"Whose phone is this?" I demanded as I held it up in the air.

Perplexity and confusion barely described the contrived and unbelievable situation.

"Whose phone is this?" I began to scream in frustration and desperation as I stepped forward, scaring everyone.

Then I turned to Katherine, "Is this yours?" I said wide-eyed and angry.

Katherine gave me that *shut-up-you're-embarrassing me* look.

"Do you want to play games, Katherine?" I roared at her. "Is that what you want?"

Even Jason tried to calm me down, but I pushed him away.

"Look!" Emma's so-called fiancé pointed behind me. "Could it be hers?"

I saw an African woman staring from behind the bushes in a green dress. She wasn't part of the crowd, but that wouldn't have made her the phone owner. I was about to dismiss her when she pointed at someone in the crowd. She looked afraid yet challenging. Her bloodshot eyes showed being yet defiance. She looked like Lupita, Deji's Najimbian admirer, but it wasn't her.

The silence had turned into murmurs. Who was she pointing at?

I followed her finger and was astonished to see it could've been anyone. Looking back at her again, she gritted her teeth at me, still not talking, then pointed back at the crowd. It was like it was prompting me to look harder. When I looked back, the best I could do was think she was pointing at the area where Emma, Katherine, and Jason stood. The place to my left.

This wasn't working, so I turned around and stepped forward toward her. She began to retreat with each step I took, so I stopped.

"Did you send me the message?" I pointed at the phone and spoke as gently and slowly as possible.

"This is nonsense," Katherine exclaimed. "Someone call the police."

Upon hearing those words from Katherine, the woman turned around and ran away.

And cross my heart, I ran after her.

I hardly remembered that I was in my wedding dress, but it

slowed me down. I must have been running like crazy because everyone else was behind me, unable to catch me, calling my name.

I followed the woman through the bushes as thorns from the plants cut through my dress. Had they cut through bare hands, shoulder and face, I didn't care. Why did anyone grow trees with sharp thorns in a wedding club in the first place?

The woman could've easily been an Olympic runner. She was unstoppable. Neither was I.

I followed her out of the garden, all the way to the club's main door. For some reason, I couldn't bring myself to call her a thief or an intruder so the security guard would catch her. Katherine would've, but she didn't run behind me like Jason and Emma, trying to help.

The African woman rushed outside, and I followed, barely thinking about the cars on the streets.

She didn't care about the vehicles, so I didn't as well. I began to call for her, "Please stop," I cried out. "I don't want to hurt you. I just want to know. Please. I just want to know."

I didn't expect her to stop and look back at me when I said that. She looked like someone who may have known Deji, or maybe I wanted to believe it true. Her eyes stared back at me, and I didn't see an ounce of darkness or evil behind them. She was only bland and silent like Tom Holmes, keeping her motives and secrets locked behind her own eyes, except that she seemed like she wanted to tell me something but couldn't?

"They're lying—" she said, almost whispering.

But I read her lips.

"They're lying!" she raised her voice this time but never finished the sentence.

A fast vehicle from around the corner plowed into her before my eyes.

And though she fell to the ground and the vehicle screeched, trying to stop a few meters too late, I saw her red blood splash on her green dress before she went down.

"Kate!" Jason cried out behind me.

I turned around with my teary eyes and open mouth, longing for his hug, swept up in the adrenaline of the moment, the confusion, the pure chaos. This was too much to take. This was...

I believe I succumbed to a fall, unlike the woman now on the ground, but I wasn't sure if another vehicle struck me.

I remember realizing that my feet had unconsciously dragged me to the middle of the street outside, leading me into a danger's path. A path where cars drove fast around a blind curve made it impossible for any driver to see or predict that someone would be standing there in the middle of the street.

17

When I woke up, I was lying in a bed, staring at a plain white ceiling. Every inch of my body ached, and I felt incredibly thirsty. I tried to move my eyes, but they hurt as well. The pain resonated deep within my bones and throbbed with every heartbeat and breath.

What happened? Where was I?

"You're safe with me now," Katherine's voice resonated next to me. I saw her jot down notes on her paper pad. "If you allow yourself to trust me, you'll find your way out of this."

Against the pain, I looked sideways and recognized her office. She sat on a chair next to me. I was on her patient's couch.

What was I doing here? I wished I could move. I wished I could sleep. More than anything, I wanted to be far away from here and far from Katherine.

"That's my girl," she said, smiling at me. It was a smile I rarely saw. Katherine never changed her attitude, but occasionally, I witnessed that generous, motherly, and a caring smile on her face, in her eyes. This look was not one I found to be trustworthy or something I could rely on. The looks were so few and far between, but I always felt that there was something more sinister beneath them.

"We all make mistakes, Kate. It doesn't mean we must keep doing them."

"What do you mean?" I finally spoke.

"I mean, Deji isn't for you," she said. "He will only hurt you."

"What?" I grimaced, trying to sit up, but my back killed me.

"He is a damaged man, Kate. This must stop."

"Why am I here?" I asked, nearly masking my desperation, yet the pain I felt would not allow me to do so. "What happened to me? Where is the African woman? Where is Jason?"

"You're safe with me. I told you," Katherine leaned forward to touch my face. "Forget about them. That child inside you hasn't grown yet. You can have an abortion. I'll help you. Allow yourself to be set free from a life of lesser things – you do not need to be trapped into a financially lacking marriage with an even more so lacking man, one who is so unfitting for you, for our family."

"What are you talking about, mother?" I demanded, startling myself to the clarity of what was occurring around me.

That's when I realized it wasn't where I was but when I was. I knew this wasn't even a dream but a cold reality from days long past. It was an old memory that had reared its ugly head to the surface. A time when Katherine thought I was marrying Deji because he got me pregnant.

I knew this was a memory because that was the last time I called her mother and then forever abandoned the title. The clarity I suddenly felt was when I woke in the middle of a hypnosis session, realizing she tried to mind fuck me into not having Andrew. This was a memory she had managed to make me forget through hypnosis. It only surfaced now when I was nearly hit by a car.

Katherine always knew something was going to happen to Deji and Andrew.

18

When I finally woke up, and not within the memories of my past, I was in a hospital bed. Jason, Emma, and DCI Tom Holmes were looking back at me. I knew this was my current reality because the aching pain ensured that I was reminded with each breath I was in the present. Real-life pain had this thing about it. It tortured you enough to make you want to hate yourself but still had this little tangent thing about it that made you think you could overcome it eventually.

"Welcome back, wifey," Jason smiled.

"You didn't make me say 'I do' while I was unconscious, did you?" I tried to straighten myself up, but Emma patted my shoulders and advised me against it.

"I don't have to," Jason winked. "You like me. I know it. We should talk about you being faster than me, though. I like to be able to catch my women. I'm insecure like that."

I wanted to chuckle a little, but I was too tired. So, Emma did it on my behalf.

"You're doing fine," she told me. "A small wound in your left leg and your right arm might stay bandaged for a while."

I hadn't realized it was bandaged until she told me. "A car hit me?" I asked.

"Was about to," Jason said. "You bumped against the passenger door." He made it sound like nothing happened, but I understood his good intentions.

"And the woman?" I questioned, needing to know what happened just as much as I needed the pain within my body to subside. Jason shrugged, and Emma looked to him for guidance before resigning to a slight shrug herself, unable to find the right words.

"She is dead," Tom Holmes said in his flat, direct nature.

"Tom," I said. "I almost forgot you were here. What are you doing here?"

Tom raised my phone in the air before my eyes and pointed at the message. In his other hand, he showed me the African woman's phone. "Ready to have a little chat?" He spoke. I nodded in agreement. Without hesitation, Tom signaled for Jason and Emma to leave the room. Jason glanced at me for permission, and I nodded back. Jason planted a small kiss on my head, and Emma squeezed my hand before they both made their quiet exit.

"Did you know this woman?" Tom didn't waste time after they left.

"No," I said. I had so many questions and so many ideas about how this conversation should've gone, but I knew Tom's attitude, so I gave him the benefit of the doubt. Maybe he was onto something. "I'm not even sure the phone is hers."

"It is," he nodded, pulling out a piece of gum from his pocket. I watched him tuck it in his mouth. An old habit, I suddenly remembered. It helped him stop smoking after a heart attack at forty-two. "It has her fingerprints on it."

"Who is she?"

"I'll get to that, but I'd like to know why she sent you this message?"

"You're asking me? Why do you think I was chasing after her?"

"Let me rephrase my question," he hardly chewed his gum but tongued it inside his mouth between sentences. "What is so special about this message? Why did you panic? What did it mean?"

"It's a children's song Deji, Andrew, and I used to sing."

"Meaning only the three of you knew about it?"

"Yes."

"Is it possible that anyone knew about it? Emma, your mother, anyone?"

"I don't recall telling them, especially not Katherine," I said. "It was an intimate, family tradition, you could say. Never had anyone heard us sing it or use the song to play together as a family. Besides, it has emotional value despite anyone else knowing about it."

"I see. But you could've also told someone about the song you sang with your kid, right?"

"I could've, but I never did. I'm sure."

"Deji?"

"I doubt it."

"But he could've."

"He could've as I said, it's unlikely, but not impossible."

"I see," he spat out the gum into the wrapper and then tucked it back in his pocket. "It could also have been Andrew."

"Definitely not."

"But it could've."

I nodded, realizing how he cornered me into telling him what he wished to hear. I still had so much to suggest, but I wanted to understand his angle on this whole conversation. I trusted him in the past. He was a good detective. He tried his best. Despite his demeanor, he did his best, and his work throughout his career led him to solve many cases, which I was so forgiving with all his many flaws. He had his methods, and I just allowed him to take the lead to do whatever he needed to do to provide me with the answers I needed.

"Do you have an idea why this woman would've sent you this message?"

I hesitated, as I didn't want him to judge me. The significant pain clouded the hesitation I was in and the swirling confusion that surrounded that loaded question. I didn't want to sound insane, but I was compelled to give him the only possible explanation.

"Kate?" He said, hands behind his back and staring out the window.

"She was trying to tell me that Deji and Andrew are alive," I said, rushing out the words before the courage to speak my mind left me.

Tom turned back to face me. His stare was long and distant, as if he were staring through me. "No, they aren't," he insisted. "But I can't stop you from believing."

"She told me 'They're lying' before the vehicle hit her, Tom," I said through gritted teeth, realizing again that I would never know why she uttered those words.

"Did you know if anyone else heard her say that?"

"I don't know. Let's ask them."

"They didn't."

"How do you know."

"I've interrogated everyone about every detail while you were unconscious."

"What about CCTV?"

"There were none at the entrance of this particular venue," he said. "Jason chose one owned by the W. They're like that with their properties. Don't ask me how they get these permissions."

"Do you ever suspect this organization, the W? I have a bad feeling about them, something just doesn't sit right with me, and this company continues to come up in my search for answers."

"I suspect everyone from A to Z, the W included," he said, knowing the stern joke wouldn't land. Instead, he probably said it to amuse himself.

"What if I told you I felt that this wasn't an accident?"

"It is an accident, Kate," he said. "We interrogated the man who hit her. He and his wife were on their way to attend another wedding in the eastern section of the clubhouse. They didn't do it on purpose."

"That's not evidence they didn't do it on purpose, Tom."

"How would they have timed it, Kate? How would they've known you'd chase the woman out to the street? Out into that blind corner, no less? It's a mere, unfortunate coincidence."

There it was again, another coincidence. I shook my head, and I said nothing. His argument was sound despite my inner doubts.

"Still, what you believe she said is interesting," he considered.

"So, you believe me?"

"Until I don't," he said. "Why would she say that? Why would she send you the message? Why would she even wait and leave her phone outside?"

"I don't know. I'm asking myself the same questions. I appreciate you being on my side on this."

"As I said before, I'm just doing my job. And my job relies heavily on concrete evidence and logic. I'm obliged to listen to everyone."

"What does the logic tell you this time?"

"Not just the logic, but the evidence," he said. "The woman's name is Adaolisa Igbo."

I straightened up in my bed against all the pain.

"She is Najimbian," he followed.

"So, she knew Deji."

"Do you know everyone who's American?"

"I wish you supported me on this, Tom. Something isn't right. It's not every day you meet another Najimbian, let alone one who sends you the song from your intimate times with your family."

"I concur, something isn't right here, but I have to use sound evidence to prove my case even though I feel the same way."

"I thought her sending me a message would stir your curiosity."

"It does."

"How so?"

"Did I tell you she is one of the suspected terrorists we've been looking for?"

"A terrorist?" My chest tightened.

"Kate, I know you just woke up from an accident, but your doctor permitted me to have this conversation with you. I need to tell you something about this woman that you will not like."

"You're not the kind of man to make such introductions, Tom. What's going on?"

"Off the record, and just because I understand your pain, what I'm going to tell you isn't something the public can know about, or it would hinder the whole case, and you'll never know what happened on that train."

"Tell me, Tom. Don't do this to me."

"Adaolisa Igbo was one of the terrorists who took your son and husband."

"That's impossible because the terrorists were Pakistani, right?"

Tom stared at his foot which he tapped impatiently on the floor, then said, "No, they weren't."

I couldn't vocalize my shock. The whole world lied to me, to everyone, about who committed a terrible kidnapping eight years ago? How could this be? After all this time, the truth was yet another mystery that I was blind to. I was half expecting Tom to explain himself, which was a dumb move on my behalf. I watched him pick up that disgusting gum out of his pocket again and chew on it as if he didn't owe me an explanation.

I tensed. "Did you lie to me and make me think the terrorists were Pakistani for eight years?"

He gripped the end side of the bed and grunted. "I'm only trying to be considerate of the pain I saw you go through, and that's because I saw my mother suffer all her life for the loss of my brother, who drowned in the river and was never found. People disappear. It happens, Kate. I've filed reports and stacks of papers and made announcements for over twenty-five years. They never returned if they didn't show up in a week's range. Most of the time, we never knew what had happened. What stayed was always the pain of the families. It goes on and on and on. I witnessed men and women fall down the rabbit hole through depression, addiction, madness, or even suicide. This hope inside your eyes will kill you eventually," he coughed as his veins showed on his neck, then let go of the grip. "All these stories in the news and papers and novels are lies. No one comes back. Death is the absence of those you love, be it physical, emotional, or someone disappearing. It has no meaning or purpose. Accept it."

"You're no different from those publications spreading hope,

Tom," I said, knowing I could've appreciated his sudden emotional ramp about what happened to his mother. But I had to push for answers. "Why did the authorities lie about the terrorists? Tell me. Tell me now!"

"That's above my pay grade," he spat the gum in the palm of his hand, as if giving up on the secret he kept inside his slightly protruding belly. "I'll risk my career, though, and give you a lead, not because I think you'll find your family members, but because I'm just sick of this," he stared at the gum in the palm of his hand as if it were a kidney stone or cancer he spat out.

Without looking at me, he said, "Two of the terrorist were in fact Pakistani. The other two were Najimbians. The Pakistani's names and identities were mentioned in the news. The Najimbians remained unknown. But we've always known they were two, a man and a woman. The woman left a fingerprint on Andrews's jacket, which was left by the seat, but we've only found her now that she sent you the message. We were never able to identify the man fully."

I took the news like an arrow in the heart, one that killed but denied me the pleasure of bleeding. No one had ever told me about Andrew leaving his jacket behind. Where did that kind of evidence go? Why couldn't Tom tell me? My mind raced as it tried to digest all this new information, the recent betrayals of the reality that I found myself in. I wanted to cry out in frustration, for once again, I found myself in front of more unending questions than I had answers.

19

EIGHT YEARS AGO...

Ouna, Ouna!

Sometimes when Deji cried in the bathroom, I stood by the other side of the door, trying to eavesdrop. I was hoping to hear him say something that would lead me to understand more.

It never worked. He was a man drenched in pain and regret. I'd begun to think that this was part of his therapy, a cathartic exorcism of childhood memories and pain washed away by the cleansing effects of water.

I've tried everything else to get to know him better in our marriage. Stories from people who knew him in the fitness space never changed the story he told me. His mother escaped Najimbia with him through the Atlantic Ocean. Najimbia, neighbored Nigeria and had a small shore that allowed the escape. Deji and his mother slept, ate, and lived under a thick sheet of plastic in a small fishing boat that smuggled them to the shores of Morocco. They took a ferry and sailed among other refugees to Europe or England. His mother was an English teacher, so she preferred Britain.

In the seven days from Najimbia to Morocco, the two remained hidden amongst the fish underneath the plastic sheets, not speaking to each other, trying their best not to breathe louder, and feeding on the rotten food. They weren't allowed to peek outside as the so-called 'pirates' who smuggled them didn't want anyone to see their faces.

Deji's mother had paid them with stolen jewelry. Yes, she stole from the rich to save her son. Sometimes the boat stopped at night for inspection by all kinds of authorities. The mother and her son could only pray that the smell of rotten fish would disgust the police and stop them from looking under the plastic sheets.

It worked.

We weren't allowed to eat fish in our house throughout our marriage. Even in his diet programs, he omitted every variety of fish. It was so evident that when confronted by clients who spoke to him about the benefits of Omega 3 and the good fats in fish, he countered science itself and denied the benefits — which came off as suspicious and untrustworthy sometimes.

That was also why he liked water, soap, and showers. It was the first thing that helped him cleanse the rotten stain off him when they arrived in the UK. Soap was an invention he almost worshipped for it allowed him to wash away the horrible stench and the physical memories of his journey thus far.

The only thing Deji's older fitness friends told me was that he had sisters whom his mother left behind in Najimbia. This had always lit a light bulb with a question mark inside my head. But I've never found an answer to it.

Why leave the girls and help the boy escape?

Sadly, his mother got sick and died right before his eyes under the plastic sheets before reaching England. It had always been a shattering story when he disclosed that he didn't even realize it until they had arrived. His youthful naivety assumed she pretended silence and stillness so as not to get caught — and because the smell of her corpse wasn't that different from the rotten fish.

In Britain, he was whisked away to an orphanage that helped refugees. He was the same age as Andrew then. Six-years-old. The connection never escaped me. What was it about this age that could lead me to an answer?

Nothing. It may have just been a coincidence.

Later in his years, Deji met lawyers from unknown organizations who wanted to help. Finally, at the age of eighteen, he realized that he had rights as an immigrant, not just a refugee. It was a blurred space, how the government treated him, and I never fully grasped it.

What mattered was his infatuation with companies like the W. Had they accepted him, whatever that meant — I still didn't fathom what they did — he would've benefited financially and lived larger.

Deji's obsession with the W's money worried me. It wasn't like him. Money typically didn't mean that much. A fact about him that I admired. He never asked to move in with my family or whether I had the right to inherit money after my father's death. He'd also objected to Katherine helping us with rent and insurance on monthly basis and accused me of being a hypocrite accepting her money. It took me some time to explain my fears of living in our country to him. How it unapologetically and systematically crushed people in their older ages.

Najimbia was another third-world African country that wasn't safe to live according to the public news. All those confusing details about the civil war, children being handed guns, and girls being raped at a young age were terrible yet inaccurate. Because at the end of the day, one would ask: *what was going on in Najimbia? Could you tell me precisely what the problem was?*

Katherine's answer to the question was poverty, ignorance, and lack of education.

Deji had as a shorter answer, "It's hell, Kate. Would you ask someone what the problem was with hell?"

My inquiries usually evaporated into thin air when I saw Deji and Andrew playing on the floor with that train at the end of the day. There were times when I deliberately stopped my tears, thinking: *you should see this, dad, you should see what I've been able to accomplish, a family, a good one, a good father, a fabulous boy. Did you know Andrew had your blue eyes? Brown skin, blonde hair, and blue eyes. And he always asked about you. He always touched pictures of you with the tips of his fingers as if trying to connect with you. I'm so lucky, dad. I want to spend the rest of my life with these two.*

The loves of my life.

If there was one thing that I occasionally suspected, other than his mysterious psychiatric sessions with Katherine, it was the absence of African friends. This one time, when we were at the movies and this beautiful African woman our age couldn't take her eyes off him.

She was so blunt and straightforward that I began to think I was invisible. Deji didn't pay her any attention, but she kept gossiping with her flock of girlfriends and pointing at him.

After the movie, coming out of the bathroom, I saw her talking to Deji. He looked upset, trying to avoid her, but she was insistent in a flirtatious way. I felt like she knew him or at least recognized him.

She left once I came to her eyesight. She didn't even look at me, let alone address me.

"Who's that?" I asked, wrapping my arms around his waist.

"She is Najimbian like me," he said and kept walking. "You know my people like to make connections abroad."

"Did you know her back in Najimbia?"

"No. She recognized me from my YouTube channel. It says where I'm from."

"You seemed a little upset."

"Not upset. I don't want to make friends with people simply because they're from the same place I came from."

"Most foreigners in this country love friends from where they came from."

"I don't like my people, Kate," he said. "Let's leave it at that."

A few days later, when I told Emma about this incident, she said something interesting to me, "Look, Kate, you know how much I adore Deji, but for a man who doesn't like his people, I'd be a little weary and dig deeper. I mean, I wouldn't trust someone who hates their own family, right?"

My eyes hung wide open when she said that, surprised by how much her words stung.

"Oh, I'm sorry," she clamped a hand over her mouth. "I didn't mean you. I'm sorry."

"Don't be. I do not like Katherine and never will," I said. "Maybe that's why Deji and I understand each other. It's just that I know why I dislike her."

"Why do you not like her so much, Kate?" Emma seized the chance to ask.

"You'll never know, sneaky girl," I smiled half-heartedly then my face dimmed. "I guess I'll never know why Deji hates his people, either."

20

Jason sat in silence on the couch in my apartment, watching me sift through Deji and Andrew's belongings. Photos, clothes, and whatever else they owned. I didn't know what I was looking for, but I was convinced that I knew what I was doing in my fit of desperation.

It reminded me of when Deji had a panic attack and decided he had to run ten miles in the cold outside. Sometimes the world made no sense; only physical activity made little sense in response.

My foot still hurt but thank God I didn't need a cane. I occasionally limped and was told that physiotherapy would make it better. It was my hand that hurt the most. Even when I refused to keep it bandaged, it still hurt if I used it, so I was sifting through it one-handed.

"Let me help you," Jason said

I didn't reply to him. I didn't know what to say. As much as he'd become dear to me, this was the worst time for talking. Something he still needed to learn about me, when to speak and when to let me be.

"At least put the bandage back on. I'm worried you'll hit your left arm into something, and the cut will worsen."

I didn't reply, realizing that I hadn't even registered there was a cut. All I knew was that the side of the car almost broke my forearm.

"Could you at least show me the woman's messages?"

"Adaolisa Igbo," I insisted. "She has a name."

"Could you please show me the messages again?"

"Why? You read it once."

"I read one message. There were nineteen in total, you said."

"They're all the same."

"What if one is different?"

"I checked them all," I glared at him. "They're all the same. I'm not going mad."

"I didn't say that."

"I think it's best for you to leave, Jason. I'm not myself right now. I don't want you to see this side of me."

"Actually, I do. I wanted to marry you because I don't mind seeing this side of you."

I pushed everything off the dining table and emptied the box of documents from under Andrew's bed, "Could you help me look if the terrorists' names were ever mentioned throughout the case?"

"Their names were Lashkar and Sipah Jafira," he said from his head. I had to turn and face him. "What? You think I didn't go over the case a million times?" he said smartly. "Do you want to know Tom Holmes's middle name? The names of the forensics on the crime scene? The name of the news channels and what was said about the incident? I know it, almost by heart. It's not only you who thinks something was wrong."

"Then why did the messages not burn your heart out as they did to me?"

"Because we promised each other to move on," he sighed, gripping the edge of the couch with one hand. "Look," he took a deep breath. "The terrorists were four. Two of them were those I just mentioned. The Pakistani. The other two had never been identified. The fact that one of the other two was a woman is a total surprise to me. The fact that they were Najimbian is another surprise to me. No one could've known because all reports described them as cloaked men with guns. They wore overhead black masks. I'm surprised you don't remember any of this."

"I do remember," I said, putting the documents down. "Only because you reminded me now. I guess I focused on clues about the other kidnapped passenger and whoever rode the train that day."

"You did?"

"Yes. I have a list of every passenger on the train that day. Until I met you, I had a list with those on the train and still rode it today," I explained. "I've even attempted interrogating many of them. Most of them didn't want to talk to me, even without knowing who I was."

"I bet they all said they've already talked to the police...."

"...and that the police themselves advised them not to talk to anyone else...."

"As some of the information is a matter of national security," Jason finished our sentence with a nod.

This moment was just another reminder of why we're probably so connected. As pleasing as it could be, love had very little to do with it.

"So, we're only left with what the news and the police reports claim happened," I said. "Four terrorists stopped the train and took nine random hostages in exchange for unnamed prisoners, and the government never complied."

"That's the story we have to live with."

"Why do we have to live with it, Jason? Why neglect the message I just received...." I stopped to his stare mid-sentence and answered myself on his behalf, "because we agreed to move on."

"Exactly," he said.

"What if I told you that when I read the message for the first time, I had no doubt Andrew sent it to me?"

"Then I'll have to be as blunt as Tom Holmes and remind you that you know it wasn't your son. That it was a woman named Adaolisa Igbo."

I took a moment and comprehended our differences. I had no possible way to explain my feelings: no one could've written this message but Andrew. There was no evidence to prove it, but like everything that happened before, I felt I was so close to the truth, yet so far.

It suddenly dawned on me that I would have to get Jason out of my life. Something was boiling inside me. Something told me that I was never ready to move on despite my initial goals. All I could see in front of my eyes was a woman standing in the middle of the street and telling me, 'They're lying' before she died in a questionable accident.

Even if I had decided to move on earlier, I'd given up on the idea. Instead, I prayed to that God that Deji believed in to help me with the rules I was about to break to find out what happened to my son.

"You know, Jason," I began. "On my way here from the hospital, I thought you would offer a certain solution to help me — us — find out the truth."

"What do you mean?"

"I half-heartedly expected you to offer to look up Adaolisa Igbo in the W database."

"What?"

"The terrorists could've easily been immigrants, right? It's farfetched that they took a plane from Pakistan or Najimbia, or wher-ever they were really from, and went straight from the airport to take hostages, right?"

"Okay?"

"So, there is a big possibility that Adaolisa Igbo is an immigrant, and the W knows something about her."

"The W isn't the only place to look for immigrants, Kate. You're mistaking it for the government," Jason seemed defensive.

"It wouldn't hurt to try."

"I could lose my job, Kate."

I was the one to take a deep breath now. I didn't like his attitude, and I couldn't shake the feeling that he knew something, "Don't you want to know who kidnapped Natalie and Mila?"

"Don't bring them into this. This is all about you, Kate."

Who are you, Jason Ross? What do you want from me?

I may have been suspicious and paranoid, but why wouldn't he offer help? It wasn't like him. This wasn't the smooth and under-standing man I had known for the past few months. It's as if my sudden revelations that I honestly couldn't, nor wanted, to move on offered me the clarity to see him on a deeper level.

"Okay, I'm sorry if I crossed the line," I had to give it another shot, "How about you talk to Tom Holmes?"

"About what?"

"Ask him more about Adaolisa Igbo. You know he wouldn't talk to me. He thinks he did all he could by exposing her nationality."

"Tom doesn't like me any better than you."

"He wants you to sign the death declaration for Natalie and Mila, right?"

"You want me to sign it in return for more information?"

I nodded in agreement. We were far from intimate people now. I guess I made it so. Our tonalities were practical and dull, and I somehow persuaded him to be as blunt and realistic as I. I could see it in his eyes.

"You know, Kate," he stood up. "I thought we would spend some time here, going over how we would overcome these obstacles and continue this thing we had together."

I was about to interrupt him when he held a hand up high, silencing me.

"I understand you want to find your family, as do I," he said. "But if you claim to know it in your heart that your son sent you this message through this woman, I know something else in my heart."

"Which is?"

He gently held me by the shoulders like Deji used to, "This is the real world. It's harsh. We've tried for eight years to find answers. You rode the same goddamn train for eight years, Kate. And it's enough."

I opened my mouth to interrupt again, but he shook my shoulders to silence me.

"I'm not saying the message is meaningless, and neither is this woman from Najimbia. And neither is the fact that Tom Holmes and the authorities are keeping a secret," he said. "I'm saying that we're small fish in this world. Even men like me with money and prestige and all that. There are corridors and floors in the W that I can't access without a pass, Kate, let alone the floor I will never access with or without a pass. There are names on my monitor screen of elite people of all kinds at work. So, I'm not blind to the fact something isn't right with the company I work for, but the same goes for the police, the government, and even your mother."

I wasn't going to interrupt him anymore. He just spoke on my behalf, telling me everything I felt but couldn't say.

"The thing is that to them, whoever they are, Natalie, Mila, Deji, and Andrew — even me and you — are disposable and hardly mean anything. So we can't face them and truly look for answers unless we break the law."

"Then let's break the law," I dared, staring right into his eyes.

He returned my look for a long minute of silence. I felt the shivering of his hands touching my shoulders, and finally, he said, "I'm sorry. I can't."

I shrugged his hands off. He looked embarrassed and picked up his keys to leave.

You're on your own now, Snowflake, my father's voice rang in my head. *But it's okay because it's not like you haven't been for the last eight years.*

"You can't because Mila isn't your daughter," I said to his back. "I, on the other hand, can't live without knowing what happened to my son."

My words hurt. I saw it in the way he reached for the door to leave. I've known him long enough to understand a few of his reactions. I wasn't sorry, though. I didn't mean to hurt him, and that was the truth. Andrew was my son. Jason never had a child. He didn't understand.

"No, she wasn't, and I feel for you, Kate," he said and pulled open the door. "If I were you, I wouldn't go as far as the W or Tom Holmes for answers when your mother probably knows much more about Deji than the police themselves."

21

Jason was right, but I knew Katherine wouldn't open up to me. Why change now if she hadn't for eight years? Besides, she insisted that the message was a prank to ruin my wedding day. Emma had backed her up this time, saying, "Why not? Someone wants to stop you from marrying this gorgeous and rich man and be happy. People are weird like that."

They were talking nonsense because if it had been a prank, Adaolisa didn't have to run or die or tell me someone was lying to me. Not to mention I wouldn't have been hurt amid the chaos either.

You can't shake that feeling, can you? My father's friendly voice returned. *You feel that Adaolisa is right. Katherine kept a secret about Deji from you. Though a good friend, Emma always came off as the least helpful when you pursued the truth. Tom Holmes is either lying or he doesn't care. You're even starting to question Jason's motives now.*

As I continued sifting through the pictures of Deji and Andrew, I came across photos I took of my father's paintings of me — the original copies were still at my mother's mansion. I had no space for them in our tiny apartment.

Tears flooded my eyes, remembering my father painting at night after Katherine had taken her anxiety and sleeping pills so he could sell similar portraits behind her back.

Why? To give them to me so I can pay the lease to the new independent apartment I lived in.

"I can't," I remembered saying to him. "These are your paintings."

"They're actually yours," he said. "Had you not been my daughter, and I know every freckle in your face by heart, you'd have been paid as a model."

He'd drawn versions of me and sold them, and I said, "I hate you when you make sense like that."

"I love you when you're not counting on being the descendant of a rich family and want to carve your own story into the rock of life."

"Your similes are cheesy, dad," I hugged him.

"I'm a painter, not a poet," he said, embracing me with the warmth of his big arms. He was a big man. I inherited my five-foot-six height from Katherine, who repeatedly reminded me that one of the reasons I liked Deji was him being as huge as a dad.

Alone in my apartment, I held photographs of what was left of these portraits. Eight of them. All the same, except the minor differences a painter unwillingly drew when copying their own image.

My father had told me about Leonardo Da Vinci supposedly having tried to redo some of his paintings, including the Mona Lisa, and never being able to replicate the same mastery. They all looked the same to the familiar eyes, but he knew only one hit the jackpot.

My father seemed to like this story a lot, so much that sometimes when I remembered it, I thought he was trying to tell me something that I didn't quite understand. Years later, Deji learned about those photos and loved them. He couldn't stop talking about it.

"What's so special about these photos?" I had asked.

Deji said, "I like the idea that one of the paintings was the authentic one. It's a spiritual thing I learned where I came from."

"How so?"

"It explains why we needed to do a lot of prayers to try our hand at something several times until it worked. It takes many prayers or trials, but only one works. Even though I don't believe in religions, this type of spirituality gives me hope and makes me wake up every day, doing my best."

A year later, my father died in prison. Had he lived longer, I wonder which levels his and Deji's relationship would've gone.

Looking at the photos now, I could see the slight differences in his brushstrokes and use of colors.

My father was a good marketeer. Part of the price his clients paid was that hanging the eight portraits of my image on their walls would have left his visitors contemplating which painting was the original. Rich people liked stuff like that.

I miss you so much, Picasso.

Andrew called him *Popa.* Papa or just Pa was Deji. Somehow grandfather translated to Popa.

My spinning head suddenly stopped, realizing my phone had been ringing for a while.

I went to check, and I wished it wasn't Jason. I didn't know what to say if he called. He was the kind who'd call after a tense conversation to make things right.

Thankfully, it wasn't him. It was Emma. Four missed calls. She was making sure I was getting better — or telling me she was fed up with her so-called fiancé. That was so Emma. She didn't leave a message, though, so she understood I needed space.

The last message was from Katherine.

A chill ran through my arms when I glimpsed Adaolisa's many messages right above my mother's.

How are you, Kate? My mother wrote. *I'm here for you.*

Even though she sounded like she was up to something, Jason's comment about her being the one to seek out answers rang true. It didn't hurt to give her one last shot and see if she'd tell me anything. She must've known something about Adaolisa Igbo.

I called her back, reminding myself to play into her emotions to get what I needed from her.

"Mum," I said. "Thanks for messaging me."

Katherine picked up. I could hear breathing. She didn't respond.

"Mum? Are you okay?"

"Yes, darling," she said. "I was enjoying you calling me mum again for a second."

"I know," I said, trying to lower my guard. "I think the event at my wedding made me reconsider things."

"You had to see someone die to consider me?"

I didn't know how to respond to that. Her logic remained as flawed as always, "I wanted to come and see you."

"See me?"

"Yes. Maybe we can talk a little."

"Are you going to bring up your father?"

"No."

"Deji?"

"I promise not to talk about them."

"I don't mind talking about Andrew."

Tears welled behind my eyes. I couldn't let her inside my head. She was a master of gaslighting and triggering emotions. She did it to test me, attempting to see what I was really up to.

"We can talk about him if you want," I played along. "I think I need to talk to someone about how much I miss him."

"I miss him, too," she said. "You want to book a session with me? It's free."

I was about to scream into the speaker and throw the phone against the wall, but I didn't. I knew she was trying to provoke me, continuing to test me so she could read through my intentions. Not to mention I had sinister intentions myself this time.

My eyes scanned my brushes stacked over the desk next to my painting palettes in the living room. Lately, I'd been drawing here. I needed the company of a TV beside me in the absence of Deji and Andrew.

My stare lingered on a particular type of brush next to a paint tube. It was a sinister thought I entertained in my mind while talking to Katherine. No one could've imagined what I was about to do, not even my old self.

"Of course, I want to book a session with you," I said. "When are you free?"

"In two hours. Take the train. You'll be here soon enough."

Take the train. Why did she mention it? I never took Deji's car to drive to her. It was always the train. But then I got it. I was about to fall into her trap.

"No, mother, I'll take Deji's car," I said with half a smirk on my face, wondering if anyone else was experiencing such a relationship with their mother. "I told you I moved on, remember? I don't ride trains and look for clues anymore."

I pictured her smiling miles away. Her silence confirmed it. I knew her *that* well. Her question was an ambush, trying to tell if the message made me reconsider my 'moving on.' Why was it so important to her that I moved on?

We're way past this, Snowflake. It's in your best interest to suspect that everyone around you is lying. Either you believe and trust Adaolisa's warning, or you don't. If you want to find your son — if he is still alive — then no halfhearted attempts anymore. You will have to break the law like you told Jason.

"I'll be there in two hours," I said and hung up, my eyes fixed on the paint tube.

22

On my way to Katherine, my mind raced through the many options I had if my meeting with her proved futile.

I certainly needed to trace Adaolisa's number. I was told it was a burner phone. Even if it weren't, its service provider wouldn't give me its owner's information, so I kept it tucked away in my mind as the last card.

I entered London, driving Deji's car, the Kia Picanto.

I'd continued paying its installment after the incident. It was an old model by now, and I rarely used it. I was glad it worked without a hassle. The hardest part was avoiding the rearview mirror as it reflected memories of seeing Andrew in the backseat.

Arriving at Katherine's gated community, full of 'renowned' doctors and physicians, I glimpse the W's high rise a few streets back. A high-rise that stood imposing over everything around it. The initials at the top looked like those in the BMW complex in London: WH: Welcome Home Inc.

I had to give it to them. Whoever they were, the name was brilliant, making an immigrant think of his new life as home. Not a new home, or even an alternate home, but just simply home.

I was told I needed a six-digit code at the gate if I had an appointment with Katherine. She worked from a large office in the house. Some clients were allowed to use the swimming pool and sleepover sometimes. They called those sessions' immersions' where they paid twice what Deji and I made in a year.

I had to remind the security at the gate of who I was. She changed security staff every three months. When I told him my name, Kate Mason, he checked the appointments and was about to let me in, but not without inspecting my car first.

I had to explain the tube of paint and paintbrush in my bag when they checked them.

"I'm a painter," I said. "I walk around with this stuff all day."

"I'm afraid we can't let you up with this—"the security man was about to complete his sentence when his partner, an older man, interrupted.

"Let her pass," he told the other. "She is Professor King's daughter. Please come in, Mrs. Mason."

I'd appreciated it if he'd called me Mrs. Olanti.

I tapped my handbag and swallowed hard as I stepped up to the mansion's main door. Katherine's secretary, a young redheaded woman, welcomed me inside.

She apologized for what happened in the train incident years ago, even though she didn't work for my mother then. I faked a smile and told her I was in a hurry. She let me in immediately.

Katherine sat on her chair next to the couch with a paper pad and her gold-plated pen. She was old-fashioned like that. Taking notes on a phone or tablet wasn't her thing, even though I knew she had her secretaries transcribe the sessions later and file them on her computer.

I nodded, trying to keep the fake smile on my face. It had to be the perfect smile, not too much, not too little, or she wouldn't trust me.

"I see you're ready for me," I said, resting my bag on the table.

The last time we hugged or embraced in person was way back. We only did it in public. There was no point in trying now.

"I'm busy," she smiled at me. I saw that she was trying to be sincere but couldn't bring herself to make it genuine. "Please lay on the couch."

I hesitated. Not because she treated me like a patient, but because it didn't help my plan.

"Can I show you something first?" I pointed at my bag.

"Can't it wait?"

"I'd rather not," I opened my bag and pulled out the paintbrush and tube. "Remember those?"

Katherine put the pen and paper aside, staring at the items in my hand, "Do they belong to your father? Because I remember we had a deal—"

"They belonged to you, once," I interrupted her, doing my best to play the part.

"Me?"

"Remember that time when you were jealous," I shrugged. "I mean, when you felt a little isolated when dad and I spent hours painting alone in the room?"

"So, it's still about him," she glared at me.

"No, I swear it's not. It's about you. Remember when you decided to give it a shot and learn how to paint so you could join us?"

Katherine remembered. I saw it in her eyes. It wasn't the best of memories to remind her of, so I acted faster by sitting on the edge of her chair next to her, hoping that forcing intimacy to a moment that seemed to end on a contradictory note would distract her.

"You see, this 'peach paint' was your favorite," I held out the tube, which looked like a toothpaste tube, ready to pop the cap. "You loved it so much."

"I did?" She said, trying to remember and not sure where this was going.

"Sure you did. Dad and I joked that you chose one of the worst brands, but you said you like it because it smelled of peach."

"I don't remember that."

"Well, it was the color of peaches, and that was how its manufacturer promoted it. But dad and I had never noticed it also smelled of peach."

"Why is any of this relevant?" She craned her head forward.

This is your moment, Kate. Seize it.

"You don't remember?" I said, uncorking the tube. "Okay, I know how to remind you. It'll come back to you if you only smell it close enough."

Katherine didn't notice that I was slowly backing away as she pulled the tube closer to her nose. She hated not remembering, and it was one of her weaknesses. In her mind, she remembered everything — and knew everything.

I did it fast. I backed away with a racing heart and watched Katherine inhale its smell into her nostrils.

She coughed right away, strangely enough not suspecting what I was doing, "It doesn't smell of peaches," she began, and she immediately saw the near-crazed look in my eyes.

I felt like the worst daughter of all time. I had no choice.

Fearing that she hadn't inhaled enough, I leaned over, and in an aggressive move, I forced the tube into her nose. The article about the paint had said, two sniffs were enough to leave you unconscious for ten minutes.

I used cheap and badly reputed paint for my devious plan. This tube was about four years old. Its manufacturer was forbidden to continue its production line after so many painters fainted because of the ingredients within the paint several years ago.

I concocted the whole story to fool Katherine.

I finally let go and watched her sprawl unconscious to the floor.

I avoided eye contact to save myself from the consequential guilt. Then I stepped back, as far as possible, when I realized I was also coughing.

23

I needn't lock the door from inside. I knew how strict Katherine was about someone entering her sessions. I couldn't bother about figuring out where the cameras were. I had ten minutes to do what I came to do. That was all.

Surprisingly, I kept coughing, even though the warning said you had to inhale closely. She wasn't going to die. All reported incidents about this product were fainting incidents or allergic reactions.

"Don't worry, Katherine, you never ever tried to learn painting," I mumbled as I sat on her desk to get her iMac to work. "You only bought the paint and tubes and let it rot while pretending you were learning to join us."

The computer turned on, but I needed a password.

It wasn't like I didn't expect that, so I began trying a couple of passwords I had on my mind, starting with her birthday. I didn't bother to try mine or dads. Katherine was all about herself.

Variations of her birthday were passwords to everything she did. She'd always said it was easier than trying to remember a convoluted password full of upper and lowercase alphabets followed by unusual characters.

I began typing.

In the past, she'd used her birthday written forwards and backward: months, date, year, or date, months, year. Written in English numerals, and she rarely used old-fashioned Roman ones.

I stopped trying suddenly. This was taking too long.

I had typed in four variations that didn't work, and I didn't know if she had installed a blocking software or alarm for too many wrong entries. If so, the computer could've shut down, and I'd had to wait even longer, wasting precious minutes.

According to what I read about the expired paint, I only had ten minutes.

Also, I wasn't feeling like myself. I didn't usually break the law, let alone sedate a family member. It was as if my anger possessed my soul, and I'd just awoke after crossing that line.

The last attempt left the screen, suggesting I use my fingerprint.

"Shit," I grunted, looking at her.

I wouldn't have pulled her to the desk and forced her up, and then used her fingerprint had I not been attacked by the image of Deji and Andrew singing our Choo Choo song.

In other words, I convinced myself there was nothing wrong with what I did.

Halfway pulling Katherine, I wondered if the password was part of the song, then I had to silence my paranoid mind. Katherine didn't take my husband and son from me — she only kept Deji's secret to herself. She couldn't have. She wasn't that crazy.

Once the computer accepted the password, I let go of Katherine's hand. The sound of her body thudding against the floor broke my essence and made me question who I was deep inside.

I gritted my teeth, wondering if the secretary heard anything, but I assumed not. Or else, she would've been knocking on the door, asking questions.

I knew they wouldn't be broadcasting live if cameras were inside the room. Katherine's clients were full of secrets, even her hypnosis methods were said to be challenging, so she'd never let anyone have a look inside until she went over the recordings herself.

My heart ached for her lying down by my feet, but I had work to do. Also, I hadn't dropped her hand on purpose. I was shocked at her desktop paper when the screen went live. It was an old picture of her, dad, and me as a child.

Maybe you're the dark one, Kate. Perhaps that's why Deji left you. Perhaps you're worse than you think you are, disguised behind the mask of victimhood.

I pressed the button on the computer, not sure who that voice in my head was. Kyle Mason hardly ever spoke to me that way.

Finding Deji's file was astonishingly easy. Katherine's folders were intricately organized. Year, months, patient, alphabetical, and so on.

I chugged in the USB attached to my keychain and began to download Deji's folder. I couldn't help but look as the process started.

The file wasn't password-protected, which was a bonus. However, Deji's folder was empty.

I began tapping my foot against the floor while I checked my watch. Five minutes to go. I speculated whether the folder was hidden or not but had no experience of knowing what that even meant. All I knew was that some people hid their files on their computers. I had a client who did that to the contracts we signed for some reason. It was deemed as a safety measure.

When the file was downloaded, I decided I needed to download the whole main folder, which was too big for my USB storage.

Why the heck was the file empty? Had she deleted it, the folder would've disappeared.

I had very little time, but I checked the parent folder labeled with the year the train incident happened.

I clicked on the file, and there it was, another file name Deji Olanti.

This one was locked.

Shit.

Like a maniac, I clicked on the parent folder and was prompted to download all of it. I had to leave soon. This was all I had.

I stood up and crossed my mother's body toward the table. I corked the paint tube back to a close and tucked it with the brush back inside my bag. There was no time to check if the paint-stained the parquet floor or the chair. I was in over my head, anyway.

Whatever consequences followed, I didn't know what to do about them.

Two minutes left.

I returned to the USB and saw that it had finished downloading. I pulled it out and contemplated whether I should pull Katherine and lay her on the couch, but time wasn't on my side.

I was about to leave when my eyes glimpsed a folder on the screen. I admit that I thought I'd seen it earlier, but my brain overlooked it, focusing on Deji's file, which I may or may not have had by now.

The file in question was in the same parent folder where Deji's information had been stored, so I had it on my USB, which was good. Perfect, exactly why I came.

Before leaving, I squinted one last time, reading the patient's name next to Deji. I mean, I never knew she was a patient. All she knew was that she was a lawyer, but there she was: Natalie Novokov.

24

Instead of returning home, I decided to drive around London.

Going straight back home seemed like a bad idea. If Katherine reported me, the police were going to come for me soon. I needed time to process what this clue I discovered meant. I had to face it. I broke the law already and had set foot in hell. There was no going back.

Lost in the gloomy city, I booked the worst one-star hotel I found on TripAdvisor's website. 10 Warwick Way in Pimlico with the most generic name ever: The Holiday Hotel. I guess reading too many Jack Reacher novels made me do this. The hotel was terrible but safe. I needed to be in the last place anyone would expect to find me, at least for now.

I booked the room on the fourth floor with the balcony overlooking the intersection at the corner. While charging my phone, I connected the USB extension and transferred the data. It would be harder for me to navigate through a phone, not a laptop, but I couldn't risk using any internet cafe by the corner. I connected to the hotel's Wi-Fi which I assumed was safer than my phone — I had already turned off my location this morning.

If Natalie, Jason's wife, was Katherine's patient, not an acquaintance, I couldn't trust them. Yes, not even Jason. I could barely trust myself.

As for Emma, I've contemplated the whole ride whether I should call her. It's not that I didn't trust her, but I didn't know if she could help.

The only one I felt I could go to was Tom Holmes, but he wouldn't tell me more. I wanted to believe I could trust him because he told me about Adaolisa's nationality. Since the authorities convinced the public that the terrorists were Pakistani, he didn't need to tell me the truth about her.

It was time to check out the files, but I had to decide whether I would answer Jason's unexpected call.

I didn't and waited until he gave up.

I tried to find out whether Deji's folder was accessible for a few minutes but couldn't solve that issue. Both folders were empty, and googling how to find invisible files didn't help. I followed the proposed steps but found no hidden files.

Before indulging Natalie's files, which I had made sure weren't empty, I ran through the other clients' names in case I recognized any of them. I assumed I'd find names of other victims from the train, so I had to re-google the train incident online to remind myself of the names.

None of them matched the other patients in the folder.

I briefly scanned through the other patients' names, looking for a connection, and came across a couple of famous politicians and celebrities. I could care less about knowing their secrets.

It bothered me that I didn't know what I was looking for. This whole puzzle was like trying to hold onto mercury at best.

Jason's wife's full name was Natalie Abram Novokov. Katherine wrote 'in some papers her last is written Novakov' in a footnote. Her daughter was Mila Novokov. Mila looked about ten. Her age wasn't mentioned. As for a husband, Jason's name didn't come up.

I searched for the word 'rape' to confirm the story Jason told me about her past. I found it. He wasn't lying. She was raped by the head police of the Russian federation. His name was blacked out with a digital marker.

There was so much to read about Natalie's past life that I had no patience to go over thoroughly. My eyes scanned her report for something that made sense.

I noticed no mention of Natalie's diagnosis. There were no transcripts of sessions. Nothing but general data.

Was it possible that Natalie wasn't actually Katherine's patient? If so, why put her folder in here?

Natalie indeed was a lawyer. Her past work at the W was mentioned. Her resignation was mentioned as well. No reasons were given.

Her daughter wasn't told who her father was. She didn't know about her mother's abuse, which I was glad for. Mila looked like she'd grow up to be a heartbreaker. She was genuinely shimmering with beauty in that one photo of her and her mother standing before.

Wait.

A train station. King's train station, London.

"Fuck this," I said. "What's with these tidbits of hints that don't ever lead to answers."

I zoomed in on the train but couldn't read its number and alphabet. Was it a single-digit or a double-digit? Which class? Other passengers stood before it.

Zooming to the right side of the photo, I saw that the sign read:

Departs: Dorchester South, 10:05, On Time

Arrival: London Waterloo, 13:01, On Time

I tried not to panic. This was the train Andrew was on. But, of course, it didn't say which day. Usually, one could continue the route from London Waterloo to King's Station from there.

The photo itself had no date on it. Natalie and Mila looked happy and were fancily dressed.

I put the phone down, contemplating everything thus far. Part of me wanted to go back and explore Natalie's file more, but I couldn't overlook the obvious. If Natalie and her daughter lived in London, why were they on a train from Dorchester to London?

What were they doing there? Did that mean they spent the night before in Dorchester? It didn't make sense.

How did Katherine have a picture of Natalie the day she was kidnapped? The only explanation was that photographer brought it to Katherine, and then she added it to the file.

Why?

Did Natalie know Deji?

I blinked to shake the idea away. I didn't dismiss it entirely, but I doubted it. Deji wouldn't have known another woman without me knowing. I wasn't going to open that can of worms. I needed to focus.

The bottom line was that two of the kidnapped people were Katherine's patients on the train. It wasn't much, but it made me feel better about hurting her. She was keeping a big secret from me, and not only was I going to find it out, but it gave me hope to know what happened to my son.

I scrolled through Natalie's file one more time. Here it was, another vague clue. This one, however, tied a few things together.

I came across another photograph. A similar picture of Natalie and Mila on that same day, almost the same pose and angle. Except that this one had someone's handwriting on it. It wasn't Katherine's. I was familiar with her style. The handwriting was two words and an exclamation mark: *Runaway Train!*

This made my heart drum in my chest. Andrew called it the Runaway Train. I thought it was just a name. Why does this keep coming up over and over again? Who wrote the note in this photo? I was positive that it was neither Katherine's nor Deji's handwriting.

I had to take a deep breath and stay calm to think straight.

Leaning back, my phone beeped again. Had Adaolisa been alive, I'd have hoped it was her, but it was Jason.

It was typical of him to resort to messages after I hadn't answered. I didn't mind his attention. Yet, I couldn't shake the feeling that something about him and his story about Natalie wasn't right.

He left me a voice message, "I did what you asked of me and talked to Tom Holmes. I bargained with my signature — which ended with me declaring my wife dead," he said in the first snippet of the message.

I watched the next short snippet load. I truly appreciated what he did, but I also worried that I had asked too much of him again.

My curiosity surpassed any feelings of regret or guilt, though. I clicked on the second message to know more.

"Here is what Tom told me. You're not going to like it. At all. That's why I wish to see you after I tell you. But, please, Kate, let's think this over and don't do anything stupid."

I already did, I thought.

I suppose my mother hadn't filed any complaints about what I did to her or made it public yet, since Jason still begged me not to cross the line.

I watched the third voice snippet load on my phone. I was eager to learn if Tom had told him about the terrorists' nationalities and whatever else he knew about Adaolisa Igbo.

It finished loading, and I clicked.

Jason said, "Tom says that the four kidnappers represented a Najimbian terrorist group. The two Pakistanis were some hired black ops. They asked to exchange the hostages with one Najimbian terrorist — not many like they told us back then. The other two terrorists were a man and a woman...."

I was about to lose my patience as he told me things I already knew, but then he dropped the final bomb on me.

"The woman was Adaolisa Igbo. The man was...," I heard Jason stutter, forcing himself to say the name. "Well, according to Tom Holmes, his name was Deji Olanti."

25

EIGHT YEARS AGO…

Deji ran into that Najimbian girl from the movie theater again. I didn't interfere this time and preferred to watch him from afar.

I was on my way to pick him up from his training studio, which he rented for free. The price? Occasionally he posed for its owner as a model for a fashion magazine. Deji hated wearing brands and tight suits, but he looked too good in them, so I understood the owner's bargain. She was one of my mother's two friends she dragged around everywhere.

At seventy and drenched in a pool of plastic surgeries and Botox, I didn't worry about her. It helped that I represented my husband as his assistant most of the time. His English wasn't up to par, and his legal knowledge was limited. I partnered with him, and thus I knew about all his clients and the times he needed to attend the studio for offline consultations.

The only part of his job that I had no control over was when he gave private massages as a side hustle. We were young. We were hopeful. We worked hard to make ends meet. Our next step was a trust fund for Andrew. It wasn't going to be much, but it was the best we could do.

I had a beautiful life. I had a fantastic life. Sometimes, I couldn't understand why or how I was still alive without them.

The girl's name was Luptia. I knew that because I read his lips talking to her outside the studio when I came to pick him up. A talent I learned from Kyle Mason himself. He claimed he learned from hours of watching people in college, trying to draw them. Later, I knew he learned it because, well, my father, according to Katherine, was a spy.

It was Deji's birthday, and the Picanto broke down, so I took a taxi without telling him. That was why he didn't recognize me inside the parked car at the curb in the middle of the pouring rain.

None of them held an umbrella. Deji and Lupita looked invincible to the cold. She looked as strong as him. I hadn't noticed she had a beautiful body last time. And though their conversation took place behind the garbage cans by the corner, a wife wouldn't miss them.

The rain prevented me from realizing the nature of the conversation. I could tell Lupita was angry. They seemed to have a connection. Was it love? Was she his sister? I couldn't tell, but she insisted on something then suddenly disappeared in the rain.

Later, I told the driver to drive next to Deji to pick him up. He wasn't surprised about the taxi and hopped in. Once he saw the package of my birthday present to him in the backseat beside me, he kissed me patiently and thanked me.

"Happy birthday, Snowflake," I told him, and he rolled his eyes, worrying the driver would think I was making fun of him. "Don't worry. I'll fix the car and bring it back tomorrow."

"It's okay," he said. "Where is Andrew?"

"With Emma."

"Cool, let's go get him and celebrate," he said, informing the driver about our next stop. "She is no one," he continued without looking at me.

"She?" I pretended I didn't understand.

"The girl you saw me talking to," he turned and faced me, looking embarrassed. "The Najimbian girl from the movie theatre."

"Oh, that's her?" I wasn't sure if I was good at playing dumb, but I did. "I thought she was one of your newer clients who hadn't registered with me yet. Maybe a massage client?"

"Not at all," he held my hand between his and locked eyes with me. "I have to be frank. She had been stalking me lately. She has that thing about being from the same place, and you know...."

"I know what?"

"You know, Kate," he rubbed my nose with his. "I told her I'm in love and that I'll call the police next time."

"As you wish," I ran the back of my hand against his wet cheek. "I trust you. Tell me if you need me to interfere."

"Sure," he smiled.

On our way to Andrew, I had to ask him this, "So you saw me in this taxi all this time?"

"You shine like a star, Snowflake," he nudged me. "Can't hide from me."

"That's impressive that you did, given you didn't look my way once. Is that some new talent I should know about?" I was gentle and fun about it, but I was also curious.

"Ouna, Ouna, Kate," he said.

"Run, run," I nodded. "You taught me."

"Yeah, but I never told you that it was the word we shouted over rooftops to the other kids when the troops came for us," he explained. "I slept in the palm of the devil's hand, so catching someone watching me was a full-time job, even when I slept."

I was thankful Katherine wasn't around, or she'd have interpreted Deji's words like something Kyle Mason would've said, thus hinting at him being a spy — or even a terrorist.

26

THREE MONTHS AGO...

I sat in the Holiday Hotel, unable to comprehend Jason's voice message. I mean, why did he sound as if he believed Tom Holmes? I was about to call him back when my door knocked.

"Who is it?"

Did someone know I was here?

"I'm a friend of Adaolisa Igbo," a girl said behind the door, border-line whispering.

"How do I know that this is true?" I was surprised I said that. I was in full conspiracy mode now, or maybe deep inside, I wished she knew Adaolisa.

"Look outside your window," she hissed. "Now."

I did and then saw a police car parked outside the Hotel.

"They're coming for you," the girl said.

"Who?"

"I don't know. I've spent my life trying to figure it out," she said.

Her English accent had a tinge of a European favor, far from Adaolisa's and Deji's. Then again, a friend of Adaolisa didn't necessarily have to be Najimbian.

"I didn't do anything wrong."

"Oh, you did. Katherine woke up furious and reported you."

"I see," I said. Did I expect my mother would let this slide? "So, I'm a fugitive now?"

"I don't know, but they'll take you in," she continued hissing. "You shouldn't have dug into her folders. Let me help you escape."

"How do I know they're coming for me? A police car driving by a low-class hotel like this could be looking for drugs or prostitution."

"That would be your lucky day if they took you in for such accusations," she scoffed. "Look, I can't let them see me. I don't even want you to see me, but I have no choice so I can show you out."

"Who are you?" I rested my hand against the door, wishing I could see through.

"Someone who's looking for answers like you."

"I don't trust you," I said, taking a step back. "Let the police come and get me. What's the worse that'll happen to a girl who sedated her mother? Let it be a scandal. I have questions and need answers. The police wouldn't tell me. Maybe if those officers take me, I'll make the news or something, and my questions will cause buzz and become public."

"I lost someone in a situation like yours and didn't find answers, but I may know a little more than you do. We're wasting time. Let me help you."

"No. Let the police get me. I want to start this fire."

"Okay," she sighed. "What if I can prove that I'm on your side?"

"I'm not stopping you."

"How do you think the police found you?"

If there was an apparent answer, it escaped me.

"They tracked your phone," she said.

"Not possible," While I didn't know much about how these technologies worked, I did what I could to cover my tracks. I had my GPS and location turned off and deliberately signed into the Hotel's WIFI. I heard stories about illegal surveillance and breaches of privacy of all kinds. Maybe, a CCTV caught me somewhere on the drive to the Hotel. I didn't care.

"The question is, why hadn't they arrived earlier?" She continued.

"Will you just spit it out?"

"Because of Jason's message," she said. "He sent you three short voice messages because his phone sent what they call a 'ping.' And that ping needs you to have your phone open for more than a minute. So the consecutive message did the job. It's the same way I knew I had to come and help you."

"Were you following me?" I said, hearing a rumble down the stairs.

"Like Jason, I did follow you, but not with any ill intentions," she began to lose her temper.

"What do you mean?"

"He probably did the ping thing to find you but didn't know the police had his phone tracked."

Though it didn't make sense, I liked her assumption about Jason. It made me feel better. He'd just signed a release paper which told me that he didn't want to help get information from Tom Holmes, or did he?

"Still, it doesn't mean Jason is an angel," she said. "He used you."

"You're playing games with me. I'm not opening the door for you."

"Stubborn bitch," The girl kicked the door from outside. "Did you ever ask yourself, how come you met him when you decided to move on?"

Her words sunk my heart to my feet. I hadn't heard the rest, but her conviction scared me.

"Why do you think he told you the same words you told no one else?" She continued.

I was going to ask how she was sure I told no one else when my tongue spelled it out for me, "Because I wrote it on my daily diary on my phone."

"Touché," she said. "He was given this data from the same person who's been tapping your phone for years—"

"How do you know all of this?"

I stood, staring at the closed door.

Your husband is a terrorist, Kate, and the man I was about to marry fooled me. Emma was dead wrong, thinking I was lucky when it came to men.

"Kate Mason?" Someone else rapped on the door in a thick British accent. "Open the door. Police."

As for the girl, she was gone.

27

It had occurred to me to jump out of the window and crawl down a pipe like those Jack Reacher novels. Even though I never had the bravery, let alone the athletics, to do such things, the injury to my arm wouldn't let me even do anything.

The police broke down the door and took me into their head-quarters while I surrendered in a haze.

It felt like a dream, as if I weren't there, much like those sessions with Katherine in the past when she hypnotized me to abort my baby.

My arm surged with pain as they cuffed me, and my leg began to numb. None of the officers mistreated me, but they were adamant about checking me in. On the drive to the station, they offered me water and aspirin in case it helped.

I was brought to sit in front of Tom Holmes, of all people.

He had closed the door and un-cuffed me. He sat across the desk, looking as stoic as ever, staring at me like an annoyed parent who lost hope in raising a better child.

"Am I under arrest?" I asked, not sure I had an issue with being thrown in jail. I felt like I could use a long sleep by now on a bed, a couch, or even a cell's cold floor.

"It's up to Professor King," he said, unpacking a brand-new gum. Ironically it smelled of peaches. "I talked to her, and we're waiting for her to drop charges."

"Which are?"

"Assault. Breaking and entering."

"Did she say anything about stealing personal info from her computer?"

"Did you?" He asked, "Because she didn't mention it."

"No, I was trying to see if she made up more accusations, knowing she'd love seeing me in jail," I had to lie, but her not mentioning the files confirmed my suspicions of a conspiracy.

"Amazing family dynamics you both have here," he tucked the gum inside his mouth. "I was about to send my son to jail for stealing from me and doing drugs once, yet I didn't."

"I have a question," I cut him off.

"Of course," he rested his hand behind his head, chewing his gum.

"How did you find me?"

"Your phone was tapped," he said unapologetically. "It has been for a long time."

"It was?"

"Eight years. Get it all out of me while I'm in the mood because I bloody hate seeing you again."

"Is that legal, tapping my phone?"

"Legal and laws are just an idea. They comfort the weak until the elite decide what to do with them," he said. "For instance, did you know that in court, most quote-unquote legal laws are usually disputable under specific circumstances?"

"I didn't know that. Like what?"

"Like if a mother kills her husband in a first-degree murder because he molested her kids; smart lawyers have ways to dispute the law, so she is not guilty and walks out. They call it the heart of the law or some bloody shit like that."

"How is this applicable to me?"

"You're a terrorist's wife, Kate," he was blunt about it.

"Is that true?"

"Deji kidnapped those passengers in exchange for his criminal brother."

"He had a brother?"

"Yes. Kejani Olanti, who is a prisoner in the UK."

"And none of you bothered to tell me his brother was a terrorist before I went on and married him?" I assumed Tom knew about me before I got married since he must have had his eyes on Deji since he entered the UK as a child.

"I'm just doing my job. If it makes you feel better, your mother she didn't know."

"How so?"

"Kejani Olanti was called Lenny Lewis to the government," he explained. "At least that was who everyone thought he was called when he immigrated to the UK. So he disguised as a music producer for a while. Then was caught for blowing up politician Jeffery Hughes while driving his car, which collided with a middle school bus on the road and killed three kids upon explosion. It happened two years before your marriage."

"But Katherine warned me of Deji. So she must've known," I argued, unsure I wanted to believe any of this. "She was his psychiatrist, for fuck's sake."

"She worked with the police and national security. Her job was to extract information by hypnosis. Authorities approached her a couple of years into your marriage."

"That doesn't add up because she didn't want me to have his child before we married."

"She probably sensed something was wrong with Deji, but the police hadn't made the connection between Deji and his brother then. Deji was under mediocre surveillance like most new immigrants. By the way, he killed his mother for trying to rat him out. She didn't pass away while helping him escape Najimbia as he told you."

Words wouldn't form inside my mouth. I didn't believe any of this.

"Is hypnotizing, even a terrorist, legal?"

"Again, it's not. There's a famous old case about the Manchurian

Candidate, a hypnotized soldier who used to commit crimes in the United States. That case made it illegal to do so, not even to a terrorist if we needed to extract information."

"So, I can sue all of you," I gritted my teeth.

"You can sue, but can you win?" He smirked, giving me mixed signals, not letting me trust him enough. "You know the number one reason most people don't sue those who wronged them?"

"I'd assume they don't trust the judicial system."

"That is the second reason. The first is that they don't have the money. Do you have any idea how much it costs to do that?" He explained. "Also, you're seven years late, and Deji is now dead. The dead have no rights."

I didn't know whether he enjoyed telling me this or if he just wanted me to leave.

"You have to understand that until the day of the kidnapping, we didn't know who he was," Tom sat forward and stopped chewing. "All I'm telling you are the discoveries we made in retrospect, and throughout the days, the terrorists contacted us to release Deji's brother."

"Who made the contacts for the deal? Deji?"

"No. Adaolisa Igbo."

"Why did she send me that message, then?"

"We don't know. The fact that Adaolisa was still in the UK puzzles me, but we'll figure it out," he said. "There is so much to unpack now. We didn't want you to know. We didn't want the public to know because many heads were going to get chopped off. You know what it means for our legal system to have been fooled by Deji, letting him marry one of us and play us all?"

"And Jason?"

"He wanted answers about Natalie. She didn't deserve what happened to her and her daughter."

"You were going to let him marry me without me knowing? Why?" I rapped my hands on the desk.

"As I said, there is so much to unpack, and it'll take some time," he awkwardly reached for my chin and forced me to look at him. It shouldn't have been acceptable, but I knew what he wanted to say. "Why don't you ask me the question you've been avoiding all day long, Kate."

I said nothing, staring back at him and letting him know that I hated him and everyone else from the bottom of my heart.

"It hurts," he said. "I understand, but you must ask me that question because that's all you care about. Deep in your core, you don't give two fucks about all the terrorists and this political freak show. People aren't who they say they are. We both knew that already. So ask me the one thing that matters the most. I don't have the best answers, but I'm here for you to blame it all on me, shout at me, and even hit me. I have kids. I understand."

I finally did, "What happened to Andrew?"

28

Tom Holmes didn't tell me much about Andrew. Instead, he announced that Katherine had dropped the charges, and that she was waiting outside in her limo to tell me all about Andrew.

Katherine sat in the back of the black limo when I arrived. I sat in the back next to her, noticing the soundproof glass separating us from the driver. I hadn't been in a car with her for ages. She used to drive her own. She used to buy a new car every year.

The backseat couch was comfy and wide, so I sat nearest to the door. She didn't mind the distance. She looked stressed, smoking a cigarette. A medical bandage ran down her left cheek. It looked like a scar she could've had from her many plastic surgeries. Oddly enough, it didn't make her look like a villain but a victim of an assault. I assumed it happened when I accidentally dropped her off the desk.

She killed the cigarette and spoke hoarsely, "Thank you for the lung cancer, darling. I'd stopped smoking years ago, but you managed to bring me back."

I didn't like always feeling like I was the one who deserved sympathy while everyone around me painted me as the devil.

And she called me darling, which meant she was back to Katherine King, not mother, mode.

"You'll be okay," I said while she signaled to the driver. The limo's glass was one-sided, so it still felt like being alone with her in the office again. "I'm not here for a long chat. Nor am I here to apologize," I continued. "I won't even ask what you knew exactly all these years or about your relationship with Deji. Where is Andrew?"

I saw Katherine suppress a smile, "You're more like me than you'd like to admit. Always have been."

"I said no fluff talk. Where is my son?"

"I don't know," she said. "We probably never will."

"Detective Holmes convinced me to ride with you to tell me this?"

"Detective Holmes wants you off his shoulders. You scare him, darling."

"I'm done with this shit," I rapped on the blocking glass and called the driver. "Stop the car. Let me out."

"Did my words offend you?" Katherine said, not even acknowledging the driver, who barely bothered to look at me.

I let go and leaned back, stretched my neck upward, looking at the ceiling, "What do you mean I scared Tom Holmes, Katherine?"

"You're scaring everyone around you, really," she said. "Why? Because you're asking questions, digging up old wounds, and you don't look like you want to stop."

"I can't believe my mother is telling me this. I tested if you were my biological mother a few years ago, and I was told you were. Why are you never on my side?"

"Because the world is built on lies, and you expect otherwise," she whispered, too close to my ears. "Jason Ross, Me, your father, Tom Holmes, Adaolisa Igbo, Deji, and even Emma, do you think they're not keeping secrets?"

"Everyone has secrets, and I don't care what they do with their lives. I care about secrets that include me not knowing about my family."

"See, that's your problem. Thinking the world is fair. We all pretend we care, but each of us has their agenda, and until your world collides with the one you thought loved you, life is all roses and dandy."

I made a fist, and my jaw hurt from gritting my teeth. I thought my silence would push her to skip the preaching.

And it did.

"You're coming home with me today," she said.

"What?"

"I'm your mother, and if this is the last time we'll ever talk to each other, I need to make sure I told all that I know. It'll take time. Besides, you haven't stayed with me at home in years."

I was weak and lost and didn't mind. I wished I could throw myself into Katherine's arms, but it didn't feel right. Something about going home to the mansion where I was raised felt reasonable now.

"I'll come, but you have to tell me about Andrew first."

"The short of it is that I don't know, but...."

"Tell me..."

"Deji must have raised him as one of his kind."

"What does that mean?"

"It means that even if Andrew is still alive, he is like his father, a good-looking, fourteen-year-old Najimbian terrorist."

"You don't know that."

"I know because I've spent years unlocking memories from Deji's head, trying to know if he had plans. At first, I was barely helping him with his trauma and past. Did you know his mother killed his father before his eyes so she could escape?"

"Why would she do that?"

"Why the bloody hell do you think I know? My job is to help with mental illness. I was trying to help him. He wasn't open to hypnosis and told me very little. Mostly about his Olanti tribe and their war against the Igbo tribe. And—"

"Wait, his family was at war with the family Adaolisa descended from? How can that be?"

She forced her hand over mine and pressed hard, "I don't know, Kate. I was trying to protect you. I've married a man who turned out to be someone else. I stood up for him against my family, then real- ized what a bad man he was," she sobbed, and it shook me. Never had my mother emoted talking about my father. *What was going on,*

Katherine? "I wanted to spare you the pain. You think I didn't suffer like you?"

I wouldn't let her drag me down that rabbit hole, "Tell me more about the Olanti and the Igbos. Do you know why two enemies would commit a terrorist attack together?"

"Deji used to tell me that his tribe had this saying, *me against my brother, my brother and I against the other, me and the other against the other's other.*"

It was hard to believe that he told her this in English unless his tribe found a genius translation for their local proverb. I got the point, though.

"So, you wanted to help until the police or government came to you, suspecting Deji was some kind of a sleeper cell?"

"Yes," she nodded. "And I didn't mind him being my trainer. The Welcome Home incorporation had told me he was good when they first let him out."

"The W?" I said. "Makes sense. They only worked with immigrants. But what doesn't add up is that Deji tried to apply for financial support while we were married, so he couldn't have been raised by the W, Katherine. You're lying."

"I'm not. Deji lied to you. He was trying to go back, not apply."

"Why wouldn't he tell me that?"

Katherine sighed, "Because it was the W who suspected him having violent tendencies. They're the ones who warned the police about him after they exposed his connection to his terrorist brother."

29

Katherine's mansion hadn't changed. It was me who did.

It felt like entering a haunted house, except one with bad memories, not the usual hauntings of ghosts or a deranged killer. Instead, every inch, every corner was a nest of memories, lies, and things I'd never forgotten.

Katherine left me to do something. I stood in the hallway, staring at the staircase leading to the second floor, where my room was kept intact. The notion tickled my heart in the worst ways. I kept Andrew's room intact in my modest apartment, and she had kept mine.

We, the Masons, were a cursed family, it seemed. It didn't matter that I left all this luxury and started a new life away from them. The story remained the same, from one generation to another. The story of a family where women marry men who lied to them, and in one way or another, took their children away from them.

I wanted to sink to my knees and cry, but I couldn't let Katherine see me like that. If I had to prove my strength to anyone, it was still her. I wasn't perfect. Sometimes, I was annoying and damaged, but I was human. Just me. I was not asking much of life but a family I now lost, wondering if Andrew's fate was my mistake.

Should I not have married a foreigner from a country I knew nothing about? It was a terrible thought, but maybe it was a mother's responsibility to weigh things differently between love and children. The father of my child didn't necessarily have to be the man I wanted, but a man I knew well and trusted, someone whose past didn't interfere with our future.

"Here," Katherine returned with a memory disk.

"What is this?"

"It's a recording of detective Tom Holmes and I, telling me about your father," she said. "I hope it still works because it's ages old, and I haven't checked it for years."

"Tom Holmes told you about my father?"

"Just like he told me about Deji. He didn't want me to keep this for national security purposes, but I insisted. I guess I sensed that I was going to have to show it to you one day."

"I don't believe my father was a spy, Katherine," I found myself saying after I've been proven wrong, time after time after time. "And I don't trust Tom Holmes."

"I'm not arguing with you anymore. I did the same if it helped. I was full of stubbornness and disbelief, and I countered every argument about your father with utter naivety. When I kept things from you, I tried to spare you the pain of having your good life and memories stolen from you."

"What?"

"Not telling you about Kyle or Deji and seeing you suffer before my eyes were hard for me. People think that knowledge will make them feel better. It doesn't. You lost your child and lived disconnected from your mother. I was trying to spare you the pain of knowing who you're father was and what Andrew's fate—"

I raised my hands and shushed her. I wasn't ready to imagine what my son grew up to be, had the stories about Deji been true.

"Your father wasn't a spy, though, but he made a living by passing cryptic messages to foreign organizations that laundered money through British banks," she explained. It was as if she was sensing I wasn't going to check the memory card's contents soon enough. "You want to know how he passed those secret messages?"

"How?" I said it halfheartedly, part of me dying to know, part not wanting to know.

"Through the paintings," she said, her veins pulsing visibly in her neck.

"You can't be serious," I said, remembering his hidden signatures in the corners of the painting and how he talked about a real one among a slew of other fakes.

"Yeah? Did you ever wonder how his shitty drawing made him any money? He had to draw you eight times only to get it right once. I know you never wanted him to feel bad and pretended you liked the images. You knew they didn't look like you even at a young age. I saw it in your eyes, wondering why he couldn't get his daughter's features right."

This one struck me like a lightning bolt.

I remember Deji saying, "*10, 9, 6, 7, 8, 5, 4, 3, 2, 1,*" teasing me because I'd numbered my father's paintings from worst to best. Deji thought that the eighth photograph was better than the sixth, thus his order. It was silly, and strangely enough, I remembered that order by heart. Sometimes when we sang the Choo Choo song with Andrew, he'd change the counting to this one where he replaced the six and the eight, only to tease me and remind me we had our secret codes.

"Why would he do this, Katherine?" I stubbornly found an argument about Kyle Mason, whom I loved with every pore of my heart. "Why would my father pass secret codes for money laundering spies or whatever Tom Holmes told you?"

"Money, darling," she rubbed her forefinger and middle finger against her thumb. "Money, money, money. And don't tell me your father had money because he didn't. You know he was bloody poor when I met him. Bloody, fucking young Katherine falling for the moody, rebellious, young, hotcake painter."

"It makes sense," I said, lowering my head.

It threw her off. I saw her eyes moisten like Jason's whenever he remembered Natalie and Mila.

"It does?" Katherine asked me, sounding genuine. "You do believe me?"

"Let me put it this way. None of what anyone told me today comes across as believable. I think you're all in on some conspiracy or something," I said. "However, none of what you told me so far is logically disputable. Yes, it all makes sense."

Katherine was on the verge of crying when a teenage girl with bright brunette hair and unusual brown eyes entered the room. I'd never seen such dense brown eyes on pale, Caucasian skin.

I hadn't time to indulge in her beauty when I realized that Katherine's emotions weren't about me. Let me explain this shuddering moment again: a teenage girl's presence in my mother's mansion was why Katherine looked so vulnerable, not because of me.

I stood amidst the two, wondering what was going on.

The teenage girl made it easier for me and went in for the kill when she looked at Katherine and said, "Mum?"

30

Katherine took the girl in her arms right away, "I'm sorry I was loud, Ella," she squeezed harder as the young Ella glanced over her shoulder to look at me with a puzzled look. "Everything is fine," Katherine reassured her.

I hadn't the strength to ask questions. Even if I wanted to, my lips had numbed. My whole body was slowly weakening, and I felt as if I would pass out. My life was one complicated and pretty much-convoluted lie. I didn't know who I was anymore.

Ella couldn't take her eyes off me. She was a curious girl. Around eighteen years old, I assumed.

Had she even known about me?

Katherine told her to go back to her room and promised her there would be horseback riding later in the afternoon.

Ella left the room obediently, and I was left in a dark jealousy bubble.

Katherine turned around, wiping tears from her eyes. How I wished she'd shown me this kind of need or longing.

"That's Ella," she said.

"No shit," I barely put the words together, fractured and cold. "She called you mum?"

"She isn't my daughter," Katherine said. "I wasn't fucking someone behind your father's back. I'm eccentric, I admit, but always loyal."

"Who is she then?"

"I've adopted her."

"I wish you'd adopted me, given how much you seem to like her."

"Don't you dare blame me," she said. "Your father took you from me, not physically, but emotionally and spiritually. I thought you'd return to my arms and give me the love I needed when Deji and Andrew were gone. Instead, you only widened the gap between us. You bloody sedated me and almost killed me in my office."

"Did you help Deji take my son from me so you'd have my love back?" Oh, how sometimes I couldn't believe the things that came out of my mouth. My life was unbelievable enough that nothing I said seemed outrageous for it anymore.

"Listen to yourself," she scoffed. "Do you think a mother could ever do such a thing?"

I changed the subject right away. I wanted to know more, "Since when did you adopt Ella?"

"Four years ago," she said. "She is my whole world."

"I can see that," I said and walked past her toward the stairs.

I should've left the house and swallowed the pain, but something deep within me compelled me to go up to my room. The feeling urged me to crawl into my childhood bed and curl up in a fetal position. To smell the sheets and let the walls of my room remind me of my past. Something in me wished that if I permitted my childhood memories to surface fully, I'd find traces of my mother's love for me as a child somewhere among them. I was okay with breadcrumbs of memory: just one memory, one hug, or even a look like she had given Ella.

"Should I count you in for dinner?" Katherine said on my way up.

"You don't need me, Katherine," I said, "I'm leaving very soon."

***

I didn't check the memory card about my father and slept in that fetal position inside my room. But I found no solace, love, or forgiveness from the pillows or bed sheets. It was odd how my childhood room felt like a stranger to me.

So odd how I changed and grew as a person that looks back at the younger me was like looking at a stranger.

I let it all out.

I cried in ways I didn't think were possible.

My body shook, my throat hurt, and tears blinded my vision. I had turned the lights off in the room and left the window open, giving way to the cold to kill me if it wanted.

Never had I cried for hours before, not even when Andrew disappeared. Because with Andrew, there was always the hope that I'd find him. But with Katherine, I failed to win her love, nor was I ever going to force myself to love her.

As for what was going on, I had so many thoughts and memories and speculations. Once I've run through all of them in my mind, I was in a blank state of emptiness. No logic, no imagery. Only pure agony filled my core, and I wished it'd crawl out of my chest and burst my rib cage open.

Exhausted; finally, my body gave in, and I slept.

**

Half-eyed, I woke up at nighttime with someone embracing me from behind.

I didn't panic.

It was Katherine.

She was crying, but her touch helped.

I couldn't quite understand why, but it helped.

In the strangest ways, she mirrored the only memory I remembered of her as a child. She was spooning my little body and singing to me when I couldn't sleep. I must've been six years old by then.

Oddly enough, the song of her choice as a child was Stairway to Heaven by Led Zeppelin.

We were two damaged women who could've at some point found a way to hang onto each other but never did.

Without saying a word, I let her hug me, letting my tears flood again.

It felt like the perfect position. I would only let her be my mother when she hugged me from behind. Face to face would've only stirred the anger. From behind, she was my mother, not Katherine King, not Kyle Mason's wife, not the woman who bought herself a substitute daughter.

It worked, but not for the rest of my life. Only for one night of good sleep, feeling wanted and unconditionally loved. After all, I hadn't slept with someone in my bed for eight years.

And little did I know of what was in store for me. Had I considered the past events insane, then I was wrong. What came after proved that all that happened to me until now was just the beginning.

31

I woke up early enough at dawn but didn't know why.

Standing by the bed, I saw Katherine sleeping. I stood staring by her for a few minutes, realizing she had closed the window that'd brought in the breeze of cold yesterday.

I rubbed my arms, noticing a bottle of pills next to her commode. Curiosity didn't entice me to check. Katherine had been using sleeping pills since I was a child. I used to hear her tell my father she couldn't sleep because of horrible stories her clients told her.

Overall, my mood was better. Sleeping usually did it for me. I'd grown to cry -- or eat -- myself to sleep many times when I realized that helped me relatively reset my life the following day.

Still, I didn't know what woke me up this early. I could've used a few more hours of temporary death.

Then I heard a melody. A faint hum as if someone was singing inside the walls.

Turning around, I speculated whether this was the reason I awoke. Like in a hide-and-seek game, I fetched the room, looking for the source. Colder, colder, colder, and here it was - warmer. Just by the window, the one Katherine had closed.

Carefully I pulled it open, and the melodies of someone playing the guitar nearby came to life.

I took a moment to check if I was dreaming, then realized that I couldn't be sure. What made these melodies real was the girl's voice singing while playing the guitar. I craned my head out and saw the light in the guest house past the palm trees in the garden. A chill ran through my body when I thought about walking down in the cold to talk to her.

Her.

My mother's new daughter, Ella.

She looked like she was smoking a blunt and playing the guitar behind the window. I knew her obedience was a facade to please my mother. What was on this girl's mind, really? To take Katherine King's money?

She looked like the typical rich, spoiled kid without worries.

There was no point in going to talk to her. Why? Was I going to get to know her? Imagining our conversation made me want to throw up.

Hi, I'm Katherine's real daughter. I mean older daughter. I mean the one who was about fifty percent her daughter. I don't think we have anything in common, and I have nothing against you. Just know that you're my substitute. That you're a filler. True, you will get her love and money, but she will take back more than you imagine. Katherine hurts people. To her, you're a trophy. I was supposed to play that part. Get out. Run away.

My darkened mind left me in peace for another chilling breeze from the cold. I took a deep breath and decided to close the window and leave in a few hours. Being here didn't do me any good. I needed to figure out the rest of my life.

Ella wouldn't let me, though.

I stopped suddenly, goosebumps crawling all over my skin, when she began singing another song:

Runway Train is never coming back,
runaway on a one-way track...

A nineties song by Soul Asylum that Kyle Mason loved the most.

Whenever he drove me around, I was allowed to listen to whatever I wanted after he played it first. Somehow it meant a lot to him.

It was a good song with a rock flavor and good lyrics. I've never listened to it on my own after my father died in prison when my mother sent him with whatever evidence she provided to the police when I was a teenager.

The only time I listened to it was after losing Deji and Andrew. It was a rainy night, and it popped in my YouTube recommendations. It reminded me of Andrew's Runaway Train at once.

I clicked on the video in a moment of weakness and couldn't believe how it accurately described my family's disappearance about never coming back. Another one of those vague clues or connections tha led to nothing.

The chances of Ella singing that song were slim. So who taught her that song?

The piling of coincidences and mysteries was getting too much and annoying. Besides, I was a terrible solver of puzzles, and my speculations were more wrong than right.

Except this time.

Ella stopped the song, and took a drag from her cigarette, and craned her neck up in my direction.

Her look was indecipherable. I supposed we had the only open windows in the mansion so early in the morning. She was staring right at me.

I watched her open the window and continue the song, emphasizing the words Runaway Train.

Then she waved at me. Was I being played by a good-looking, mischievous teenager? Was she nothing but a cruel version of Katherine?

She won't wake up before the hour, Ella mouthed to me.

Shivers ran through my existence.

Ella also knew I could read lips. Only Kyle Mason and Deji knew that.

I turned back to look at Katherine. She looked like she wasn't going to wake up anytime soon. Ella was right.

When I turned back, I saw her mouth the words I wanted to read. Deep inside my core, I wanted someone to repeat them to me.

They're lying, Ella mouthed.

I ran down the stairs, hoping I'd reach her before someone killed her like Adaolisa Igbo.

32

"Shut the door behind you," Ella said, all business.

I did, watching her pull the curtains down and dim the lights. The young kid seems to have a plan. I didn't know who she really was, but I followed her instructions.

She pointed at the bathroom.

I entered, glimpsing her put on a loud record before following me.

Even in guest houses, rich people's bathrooms were big enough to host a party. God, I couldn't believe I spoke as if I wasn't one of them.

"He is alive," Ella said.

"Who?" I again stuttered in a one-syllable word, wishing she would tell me what I wanted to hear.

"Andrew Olanti," she said, closing the door behind her.

"How do you know that?"

"Let me help you before the police, or whoever is coming for you, arrive again."

"You're the girl from the Holiday Hotel," I shrieked.

She cupped my mouth with her hands and titled her head as a warning.

"Okay," I muffled out the word. "I'll stay quiet."

"Good," she said, pulling away. "And yes, it was me. I was trying to spare you the lies."

"So, it's not true? Deji isn't a terrorist? Is Andrew alive? Where? How can I see him?"

"I'll forgive you for asking more and more questions," she lit up another cigarette and then took a long drag from it. "Want some?"

"No, thank you," I shook my head, obedient. If I wanted answers, I had to slow down and listen.

She pulled a pen from the drawer next to her and wrote on a napkin with the cigarette in one hand—a couple of sentences with numbers.

She folded the napkin and tucked it in my hands, pressing on them while the cigarette hung puckered between her lips, "Take this."

"What is it?"

"I'll get to that," she said. "Just keep it in case I'm killed or anything."

"Are we in danger?" I said, then clamped my hands over my mouth. "I'm sorry. I'll shut up."

"A slow learner, aren't you?" she said. "So here is the deal. I don't know what everyone else told you. They surely told me lies as well. They're good with making up things and piling up lies. What I know is that Deji isn't a terrorist and that Andrew is alive."

I didn't speak, but my eyes did because she continued, "He is not being raised as a terrorist, and he is not hurt, nor was he ever."

I lowered my hands, "I'm so happy."

"Stop the tears and sappy cliches," she said. "I will tell you where to go and whom to meet to get your final answers."

"Please do."

"You have an address on this napkin. I have the Corvette Katherine bought me for my eighteenth birthday - and my one million pounds trust fund — right outside the guest house. I keep spare clothes inside, so Katherine doesn't know I spent the night outside. You're almost my size. Take the car and leave. I'll open the gate for you because you need a code otherwise. Once you're out, park the car anywhere and get a taxi, not an Uber."

I listened intently. Who was this girl?

"Take this," she pulled out a phone from her pocket. "It's a burner phone someone bought yesterday. I stole it from them, which makes it a stolen burner - hardly traceable. Use the phone and call the number on the napkin. The man on the other line will send you a location near the address because he is in deep shit himself and can't know where it's best to meet you."

"Is he going to tell me how to find Andrew?"

"He is going to tell what happened to Andrew and Deji. I know what happened, but he tells it better because he knows the details and the bigger picture — and probably what to do next to find your son."

I didn't see how I could force her to tell me what she knew right now. She was the badass I wanted to be as a teenager.

"Now, to put things in perspective," she killed the cigarette on the floor, "Do you know who I am?"

"No."

"Think."

"All I know is that you warned me from the police arriving, and you warned me of Jason."

"I didn't warn you of Jason Ross. I told you he tricked you into locating you, but he didn't know they had access to his phone."

"Whatever that means, I don't care."

"How do you think Katherine found me?"

That was a good question. Where did Katherine go to adopt someone? The answer was on the tip of my tongue, just as Ella told me.

"The W," she said. "Where better to get an immigrant to play her substitute daughter?"

"You don't have the slightest of accents."

"I was born here. My mother is an immigrant. Besides, I needed to play my part."

"What part could push you to sacrifice the best years of your life to Katherine?"

"I'll answer this in my next question: who in the W do you think recommended me to Katherine?"

"I only know Jason Ross from the W—" I swallowed hard. "It was Jason who recommended you? Katherine and Jason knew each other?"

"Not personally, but he represented the company."

"I see."

"Why do you think he did that four years ago?"

"You're probably his only way to find out what happened to Natalie. I'm starting to think he knew Natalie was Katherine's patient and wanted to investigate her files."

"Good, but the files, which you and I read, don't have much to them," she said. "Jason needed me to gain Katherine's trust to get into her lion's den, figuring out what happened to Natalie and probably everyone else on the Runaway Train."

"Runaway Train? What do you know about the Runaway Train?"

"It's a train, not only from Dorchester to London. It has many routes. A special train like no other."

"I'm not sure I'm following."

"You will know all about the Runaway Train when you meet that man."

"Okay.... but how could Jason do this to you? How could he use you to his benefit like this? What does he have on you? Why did you agree?" I was spurting questions out of my skeptical head, caring less about her advising me against it. Was Jason Ross the devil himself? First, approaching and making me think he loved me, then convincing this girl to play that part with Katherine?

"He didn't make me do anything," Ella said. "I asked for it."

"Why?"

"Take this," she clamped, a physical photo turned upside down in the palm of my hand. "I promise it's the last thing I'll give you tonight."

"Should I turn it around?" I pointed at the photo, trying not to sound nervous.

"Only when you're in the car. Just remember the magic of dying one's hair and wearing contact lenses. You'll need to remember this because people aren't who they seem to be, but sometimes that is good."

This last sentence didn't resonate with me, though I watched her point at her hair and eyes.

She took a moment to look at me. I didn't understand why or what she was looking at in my face. "I hope you find your son. Unfortunately, I failed to find what I was looking for."

"What is it?"

"You'll know soon enough. The man you're about to meet will explain it all," she said. "I have a feeling you can make it. Of course, the world will be against you, but I think you can make it. Now go."

She pulled open the door and guided me through the backdoor of the guest house. When I tried to say goodbye, she pushed me, afraid to get emotional.

"Promise me you'll come and save me if you find your son," were her last words to my back.

I stumbled in my run, confused whether she wanted to say more or if I should've turned around. She had closed the door already. I had no time to waste.

I got into the Corvette. I knew how to get it up and running. After all, I was a spoiled, rich kid once and drove many of these cars. I checked her bag of clothes in the passenger seat and decided I'd get dressed once I left the mansion. To my surprise, I found my ID and keys to the house in that bag.

I guess it wasn't my mother who closed the window in my room. It was this crazy girl. She'd planned it all.

I took a deep breath and turned around the photo she gave me.

I'd seen it before. It was the original photo of Natalie and her daughter standing in front of the train on the day of the incident. I supposed it was the girl's handwriting that said Runaway Train on the corner.

That was all, and I didn't know how this explained who this girl was.

I turned the photo around. There it was.

A full message Ella wrote for me:

When they took my mother, I became Ella. From blonde to brunette, from blue to brown, naive to wide eyes, and innocent of growing up. So when you find your son, find my mother, then find me.

Yours truly,
Mila Novokov.

33

The address Ella gave me was near the W. Two blocks around the building close to my mother's gated society.

I paid for the taxi in cash, dressed like a businesswoman in an area full of businesswomen. Ella, I mean Mila, thought this part out as well. I needed to blend in.

I still couldn't get that girl out of my head. What kind of badass gave away four years of her life to find her mother? I knew Mila was Russian and heard that girls there had a certain sense of resilience, but I could never imagine how she brought herself to do it.

What Ella did worked, or she wouldn't have found the contact I was supposed to meet now.

Many other questions arose, like why didn't Mila's contact find her mother or why Natalie disappeared on the train.

The biggest question of all was how did Mila return? Wasn't she kidnapped on the train as well?

What mattered the most was her promise of Andrew being alive and well. For someone who did what she did, I believed her.

The contact sent me a text:

11 am, at the Imperial College Cafe. Don't contact me again. Just be there. I know what you look like.

It was 11 am already, and I waited for my mysterious contact inside the cafe.

I'd ordered coffee and sat by the last seat next to the wall, facing the window. I bought four big coffee cups and a ton of bagels in a carton, and I left the highchair next to me. I didn't want anyone to sit next to me, and the contact needed a seat.

My phone vibrated. I thought I'd keep it silent to avoid attention when it beeped. Another text:

Usually, I shouldn't call you, but I will. You'll understand why in a sec. Please don't do anything stupid. If you trust Mila, then you can trust me.

The last thing I needed was for the caller to be as dramatic, but I wasn't here to judge. *Just tell me where my son is.*

The phone vibrated again, and I picked up right away.

Trying to be more cautious, I said nothing. I wanted him, or her, to speak first.

"Kate, it's me," the voice said.

"I don't like this at all," I fired back, then lowered my voice and bent over the counter with an angle toward the wall.

"Keep calm," the man on the phone said. "I'm not as bad as you think I am."

"What are you doing here?"

"I'm your source. Mila didn't want to tell you, so you would accept me helping you."

"How in God's name do you think I'd trust you again, Jason?"

"We don't have time for this," he sighed. "I really like you, if that even matters to you."

"Is this a joke? Where is my son? Who are you working for?"

"I told you that I work for the W. I'm just a man who lost his loved ones like you," he tried to keep his voice low. Where was he? "But I didn't trust anyone, not even you. I understand that people are two-faced and that confrontations and asking lead to nowhere, so I agreed with Mila's plan when Katherine asked the W for a teenager to adopt."

"You make it sound so noble when you made a teenager give away the best years of her life."

"She wanted it. She had only Natalie. She was born to a man who tortured and raped her mother, and she wanted to go back to Russia and kill him. She had so much anger inside her. It gave her purpose," he said. "Mila and I wanted to find out the truth, and you won't believe what we know so far. We only can't act on it before we find our loved ones."

"Had you known enough, you wouldn't have come for me, Jason. I think your plan with Mila failed, and since you didn't trust anyone, you came for me, smoothly sliding yourself into my life and pretending you cared."

Jason didn't reply right away. This gave me a moment to crane my neck to see if he called from inside the cafe. Also, to make sure I was far enough from anyone to eavesdrop.

I couldn't find him anywhere.

"I'm sorry for what I did, but I thought you knew," he said.

"Knew what?"

"I thought you knew what happened on the train and weren't telling me."

"What the fuck, Jason," I said, a little louder but then controlled my voice again. "How did you come to this genius conclusion?"

"Don't take it the wrong way, Kate, but I couldn't imagine a son being taken from his mother without anyone telling her."

"The same thing happened to you."

"Mila wasn't my daughter. I only stumbled across her a week after the incident."

"Now stop right here and explain to me how this happened."

"They found Natalie after the day on the train, so she protected her daughter by sending her to the W and giving her a new identity. Natalie had to start all over again on her own. We don't know if she's alive."

"I don't understand a thing of what you said."

"You won't understand before I tell you about the Runaway Train."

"I'm listening."

"Straighten up first and face the window."

"What did you say? Where are you?"

"I'm in the cafe across the street, sitting by the window as you, but I'm not facing you. I'm facing the curb. You'll be able to see me sideways."

I did as I was instructed and saw him. He talked to me from a headset and faced an open laptop, pretending to be working. It didn't suit his look to be working on a laptop in a cafe at all.

"Why can't you talk to me face to face?"

"Remember Adaolisa?"

"Are you risking your life by doing this?"

He nodded without looking at me and said nothing.

"Then tell me before something happens to you," I said bluntly, as if I were Tom Holmes.

Jason smiled bitterly from the corner of his mouth as if he'd already signed his death sentence.

"First of all, you have to know that I didn't know about Adaolisa when she sent you the message. It surprised me as much as it surprised you."

"I'd like to believe that. Go on."

"Also, you have to know that I'm just an ambitious man who worked for an overly ambitious company, the W. Before meeting Natalie, immigrants were just the job I had to do to get paid. And they paid heftily. I was a selfish man who never questioned the firm I worked for before I met her."

"This is the first time I believe you since I've met you."

He let out that regretful, bitter smile again.

"So, the W is behind the train incident eight years ago?" I speculated.

He nodded without answering, knowing I saw him.

"The W kidnaped Deji and Andrew?"

"No, Kate," he said. "They saved them."

34

SIXTEEN YEARS AGO

Kyle Mason was on his seventh painting of me when I entered the room. I was fourteen years old, having dabbled with painting just a little.

He was so consumed by his work that he didn't see me, so I stood back and watched. Whatever he did seemed meticulous and took all his attention. He was using a thin brush and worked on the lower right side of the painting. I couldn't understand what he was doing since it seemed like he was drawing something almost invisible.

I silently got closer.

This time, it seemed even stranger. He was using a thin black brush over a dark patch at the lower corner of the painting, at a part, no one cared to look. It showed the black dress he imagined me wearing, and it made no sense to work as hard on such a part.

"It's my secret sauce," he said, hardly surprised at me watching him in silence. He didn't look like he was hiding something at all.

"Secret sauce?" I said with bulging eyes. "Can you teach me?"

"Nah, you're too young," he teased me. "One day, when you're older, I will show you. I think you will like it."

"The secret about the secret sauce?"

"No," he said, smiling, "I'll teach you what the secret sauce means."

"You're confusing me."

"Don't worry about it now. Always remember what I told you about the future and past."

"Of course, I remember. The past is always true because it happened, and we know it happened."

"And the future — sometimes the present — is only lies until it becomes the past, and we know it happened."

"You've told me too many times, dad, I remember."

"I didn't tell you this last part, though," he said. "When the older we get and step into the future and make our present our past, it sometimes leads us to an interesting conclusion."

"Which is?"

"Sometimes, the past is the greatest lie of all, even though we saw it happen."

35

THREE MONTHS AGO...

"You're not making sense," I told Jason.

"As Mila told you, Deji wasn't a terrorist. He didn't kidnap passengers on the train, but he wasn't kidnapped either."

"Enough with the puzzles."

"It's not a puzzle. Your husband, and my wife, rode that train eight years ago, knowing that they weren't coming back."

"I don't believe that," I said while remembering the look on Natalie and Mila's faces in the photo. The look of happiness to getting on the train.

"Get over what you believe and what you don't. I have something for you that is indisputable evidence of my claim," he said. "Natalie and Deji and the other so-called kidnapped members got on the Runaway Train willingly that day."

"Does that explain the picture of Natalie and Mila in front of the train? I've always wondered why they looked so happy about it. I always wondered why Natalie, the rich lawyer, took a train in the first place. Why she didn't book first class and be in the same car with my son and Deji."

"That's because the train was her savior from the past. It was her only way out from the Russian mob who hunted her, and from the man who raped her because she was about to expose his corruption in Russia."

"What about Deji and Andrew?"

"Deji was like Natalie. His past was after him, and they wouldn't leave him alone. He knew he would wind up dead or that they would end up hurting his family."

"The past that he'd never told me about," I said absently, wanting to believe this version of the truth. It struck me as right so far. "What is a Runaway Train, Jason?"

"An unspoken savior provided by the W, one that some governments approve of, and others don't," he explained. "Let's put it this way: imagine you're an immigrant from a country that isn't crazy about human rights. A country where most atrocious tribal madness forces them into civil wars and blood. At the same time, it's a country rich in natural resources, be it oil, gold, or human trafficking, all of which are so valuable to the West."

"Okay?"

"Then imagine that you, like Deji, left to find, not necessarily a better place, but one that applied modern laws and logic to how it treated people. A country where relatively your race and background and ancestors didn't stain your hands with blood."

"You're describing my husband in detail. I imagine this was why he cried and had his panic attacks."

"Then you realize the unholy, the unexpected, and unbelievable," he said.

"Which is?"

"That no matter how far you went, your past won't let go of you, and that the people you've got involved with and loved are now stained with the sins of your fathers. That you have put them in great danger."

"I'm beginning to see where this is going, Jason. I believe you," I said, trying to hold my tears, wondering what he would tell me next.

"I don't know what Deji's past story is, but I know Natalie's," he said. "The Russian mob found her in London and began threatening her. We're talking about telling her they will hurt Mila, and you know what they already did to her in the past. If she wanted to live in peace, she had to forcefully immigrate illegal Russians into Europe."

"I assume Natalie asked the W to get on that Runaway Train?"

"Not exactly. That's not how the W works. As a front, the W helps immigrants get into the country, not out. It works with the British authorities and files legal papers and pays taxes. It has stockholders and contributes to charity and no one suspects otherwise."

"Ahh, so the Runway Train is their untold secret," I said, almost thinking. "Are you telling me the W is the good Samaritan hiding among the elite without them noticing?"

"Not a bad way to put it, but yes," he said. "And there are many. In London, Liverpool, Birmingham, and in almost every country in Europe. I've heard they branched to the states, but I'm not sure."

"How didn't you now know any of this when you worked in the W?"

"Because I was the greedy employee in the perfect suit with the perfect looks. I was one of those the W used as a front. They never trusted me until Adaolisa started a chain reaction with the message she sent you. Mila caught Katherine talking to Tom Holmes about the Runaway Train and the W, so I began breaking the rules and found out all about the Runaway Train. The picture you found in Katherine's office was so recent. Mila sent it to me to tell me about the Runaway Train and that it existed. Katherine found out about it but thankfully didn't recognize it was Mila's handwriting — at least so far."

"That's why she asked me to come for her if I found Andrew," I said in a fractured voice.

I needed more time to let things sink in. Jason's story felt like it missed something, especially the parts concerning him, but I reminded myself of my end goal: finding my son.

"So, how do I get my son, Jason?" I said. "Where did the Runaway Train take my husband and son? What was Deji running from, and to where?"

"I don't have the answers to that, not even to where Natalie went. I imagine they're taken into something like witness protection program, sent to live in a faraway country, under new identities," he said.

"Still, I can't imagine Deji didn't take me with them. Why would he not tell me? I'd have gone with them to the end of the world."

"I've thought about this a lot, and I haven't figured out an answer to that question, Kate. I'm sorry." He said, pity in his voice.

"But Mila must know. She returned?"

"Mila's story is that the so-called terrorists covered their heads in bags and drove away. After many trials and errors, she recognized the kidnappers languages were Pakistani and Najimbian. She recalled Deji not saying a word, but Natalie had a long argument in English with them."

"What was it about?"

"They told her that they had no place for her daughter and that she wasn't in danger if sent back to the W. Natalie whispered to her daughter that she couldn't take her along and that she would drop her off at a safe place in the W."

"Why not do the same with Andrew?"

"Mila said that she sensed that Deji wasn't just protecting himself by taking the Runaway, but also Andrew."

"Why would his people want to hurt Andrew?"

"I don't know," Jason said quietly.

"What did Andrew say when their heads were covered. Did he ask about what was going on? Did he know this was going to happen? Did he ask about me?"

"I don't have much time," Jason said, looking over his shoulder. I squinted to see if he was in danger, but none of the people in the cafe came off as suspicious. "All I have for you is a video taken in the W a day before the incident," he shyly waved another USB next to him without looking at me.

"Send it to me."

"It's encrypted."

"I'll come and get it," I said immediately.

"I don't want you to be seen with me. I sense I'm in danger. I don't know the dynamics inside the W, but not everyone in there likes their strategy. No one is supposed to expose the idea of the Runaway Train," he looked like he was contemplating whether to turn around and look at me or not. "I'll leave now and leave it at the desk behind me—"

Jason was too late. I didn't hear the bullet but watched his head bob and his body snap, then drop to the floor.

36

The man who shot Jason was African. I could spot him easily — the only person suspiciously calm near him. I watched as he carefully stole the USB from the floor and tucked it in his pocket while everyone around him screamed in panic. He didn't visibly carry a gun and probably shot him with a silencer. I couldn't tell for sure. In a vain effort to blend in, he acted as if he was checking on Jason, yelling for an ambulance.

I rushed out of the Imperial Cafe and around the curb with my eyes fixed on him. I bolted across the street, never losing my gaze. Any vehicle could've ended my life like Adaolisa, but I had nothing to lose. I was after the USB the man took.

Adrenaline fueled my engine, and I ran faster than I ever thought possible.

None of the pedestrians I passed dared to stand in my way or question why I was running. As I approached the other cafe, I saw the man leave from an exit door farthest from me. He wore a business suit, but his overall appearance wasn't as put together as Jason's. He looked more like a bodyguard, well, a hitman. A huge man built even more potent than Deji.

My mind told me to scream at him and ask him to stop, but I

knew that it'd only prompt him to run faster. The longer he didn't suspect I was coming, the better.

The speed of my run was suddenly interrupted by the appearance of a pregnant woman on the sidewalk. I knew I would be forced to go around her, so I didn't cause any harm. I looked ahead and realized I would need to deviate from my path for her safety. While only a few seconds, the delay was haphazard for my once-promising closing in on this dangerous man. When I reoriented to my target, I realized the loss was damning. He was getting inside a car.

Fuck me.

I suddenly felt like I could take things into my own hands for the first time. I felt overcome with power, fueled by adrenaline, desperation, and a little revenge. I would have never imagined I had such a strong will to get that USB in the past. I saw a man placing a coffee on the roof of his car as he was putting his keys into the door to unlock it. I knew it would be my only chance. I forcefully bumped into him, watching as the hot coffee spilled over his chest. He yelled profanities and stepped back while I seized the moment, pulled the keys from the door, got inside, and started the engine.

Not that I gave a damn, but he probably thought I was insane.

I pushed the pedal and blindly pursued the mysterious car. Nothing showed up in my peripheral vision. It didn't matter now. I used all my focus on the escaping vehicle before me. No way I would catch the African man without hurting a pedestrian. It was wrong to be so irresponsible, but as Katherine said, everyone fought for whatever they wanted and rarely cared about the rest.

It crossed my mind to drive up the pavement like in movies to catch the man, but I wasn't that selfish or desperate yet. I slammed the horn like a madwoman to get people out of my way, my eyes never leaving the car. I accelerated even more, and my mind drifted back to Jason getting shot.

What was going on? I thought. *When did life become so complicated and disgusting?*

I thought about Mila telling me to come and get her if I figured out the truth. She must've known that Jason wasn't going to make it. I promised myself to come back for her if I survived this situation and found my son.

The car chase wasn't getting me anywhere. I didn't lose sight of the man, and as much as I liked to think I was driving like crazy, I didn't seem to bother the other cars in my path. Driving in London was mad enough on its own. I decided to push the pedal harder and rear-end the car I was chasing.

As I was close enough, I decided that rear-ending him wasn't good enough. Instead, I took a steep left, cars honking at me in anger as I went against traffic. Just as I was parallel to his car, I sharply turned the steering wheel back to the right in one final motion.

I plowed in the middle of the car's backseat and hit my head hard due to the sudden impact.

Blood dripped from my wound, but I forced myself to stand up and get out of the car. People panicked around me, unsure whether I needed help or the police. I guess I made their day: a murder nearby and a car accident within minutes.

It surprised me how much damage I caused to the other car. I saw the black man spitting blood through the broken window while his legs were trapped under the mess the backdoor had become.

I knew where he'd tucked the USB, but I found myself limping as I approached.

Come on, Kate. You're so close.

I ignored my limp and the pain in my arm that grew stronger. *Why didn't I keep it bandaged so it'd have gotten better by now?*

I went around the car to get inside from the undamaged door. I opened it, listening to people hissing about the crazy woman drenched in blood. Soon the police sirens would sound. Jason's death down the street must have occupied the police for a while, and whoever was driving this car had escaped already, but he didn't matter. I let him run away because the only thing that mattered was the USB.

I didn't even speak to this African man while I reached inside his pocket. Once I caught hold of it, he began spitting blood again. He didn't have the strength to muster up a fight.

I should've fled immediately, but he seemed to say something as I turned to leave that I couldn't make out.

"Who are you?" I said, my limping leg already halfway out of the door.

"Ig," he spat blood, and slowly I realized he was dying. I realized that I had just sent this man to his death. "Igbo."

"What about Igbo?" I growled. "You know Adaolisa?"

"Igbo."

"Tell me more!" I shouted. "Why did you kill Jason? Where is my son?"

And then he uttered his last words, "Ouna. Ouna."

The sirens sounded in the distance, and people began pointing at me. I was already deep into this mess, but by no means did that mean I had to give in. I'd seen the gun he used to kill Jason on the seat next to him, so I leaned back in and picked it up, knowing he had no further use of it.

Not even knowing how to use a gun, I still aimed it at the public. "Whoever is going to stop me will die," I screamed, not recognizing my own voice.

What the hell are you doing, Kate? Who the hell are you?

In a usual scenario, the police had to get me sooner or later, but I didn't know whose side the police were on anymore.

My eyes caught a couple of students with laptop bags as I began limping away. I preferred not to think of the consequences as I pointed the gun at one of them, "Give me the laptop. Now!"

"Okay, okay, lady," a wide-eyed young student said as he handed it to me. "It's second-hand anyway."

37

Running with a limp was a task I thought to be impossible, but the adrenaline pumped through my veins and fueled my soul. I entered a random building near the crash I had just caused. I wanted to take the elevator upstairs to the roof, but it would take too long.

Limping up the stairs wouldn't help either, so I rounded the corridors and dizzily knocked on an apartment door. I threatened whichever poor soul opened it with my gun.

I no longer saw people as human beings but more as obstacles standing in my way. None of the faces that stared back at me meant anything to me.

"Where is the bathroom?" I yelled, pointing my gun.

The terrified residents cowered together. A woman in the back of the room stood before her two sons, protecting them from me. The younger teenage boy pointed me to the bathroom.

I got inside and closed the door behind me. Soon the police would come for me, but I had to see the contents of the USB first.

I plugged the USB into the second-hand laptop, which was miraculously unlocked. I clicked on the USB location and found one file inside: a video named:

Welcome Home Inc., Client 237, dated eight years ago.

When I clicked play, I saw Deji's face.

38

I only saw his upper half, sitting in front of a white background. He wore an unusual white costume that reminded me of the official Muslim Pilgrimage outfit. While it reminded me of the traditional garb, I knew it wasn't quite the same as I looked closer. It looked like he had wrapped himself in a white shroud and bared his shoulders.

I squinted, and I saw that the video was recorded a day before the train incident, as Jason told me.

The W's watermark logo was present in the left corner of the video. I began watching...

Hello, Snowflake, he began, smiling at me as if he could see me through the eight-year-old screen.

If you're watching this, I assume seven years have passed.

He swallowed hard, probably realizing how this pissed me off more than made me happy. He then raised his hand and touched the screen with the tips of his finger as if trying to touch my face.

If it's true, then you'll be watching this after I'm declared dead.

In this case, I, Deji Olanti, have no words to compensate you for the pain you've been through. I'm as guilty as charged, not with doing the wrong thing and neither the right thing, but doing my best considering the circumstances.

I wiped my tears, thinking of fast-forwarding to whichever part he would mention Andrew. I suddenly hated Deji so much right now. What excuse did he have for what he's done to me?

Andrew is fine, I promise you, even if seven or more years have passed by the time you're watching this. If you know about their involvement by now, the W are good people.

I can't in a million years explain why I took our son away — away from you. All you need to believe is that I was a danger to him, he was a danger to you, and you couldn't have come with us, or they would have killed you.

He sighed, trying to make sense of his words.

I'm sorry to tell you that I can't confess, not even now, why I did what I did. If I tell you in this recording, you won't have much time to live.

Since I'm talking to you from the past, I don't have the answers to what happens next. Believe me, Snowflake, I didn't know they would find me. It wasn't even an option, but I can't explain why now.

I was supposed to be done with who I am, who they wanted me to be. But then something happened, and I had never thought of it.

And when it did, there was no way to stop them.

Anyway, this is why I recorded this video. I'll explain several precise points.

One: now that both Andrew and I are officially dead, they're not going to look for us. They trust the British system and think they know what they're doing. They don't understand that we live in a world where you're declared dead for being absent for so long.

Two: Andrew is safe and will be raised properly. He will always be your son, and I love you so much.

Three: I, however, might be dead by now.

He stopped and looked down, then raised his eyes at me again.

I hope I'm not, but it's possible.

Four: This is the reason for the video. To find Andrew, you have to find my wife.

I stopped hiccupping with tears, all ears now, not as shocked as I'd have been a few weeks ago.

Yes, I was married before you. You should be able to understand later, not necessarily forgive me. If I tell you her name, it'd be a risk. I don't know if this recording will end up in the wrong hands.

My wife is the only one who knows where to find Andrew after seven years. She vowed to help. She vowed to pass the secret to her daughter — no, not mine — if she died. The bottom line is: you find her, and she tells you why I left and tells you how to get to Andrew.

He pulled the camera near his face and spoke with conviction.

From now on, you can't trust anyone. I know you might have been told this already, given that I know how relentless you are about finding the truth. But this is a different thing. I'm telling you: only to trust my wife.

"I will," I spoke to him, hardly paying attention to the police officer outside my door, threatening to break in. "Just tell me where I can find her."

Again, since I can't tell you her name, you will have to get it from detective Tom Holmes. Yes, him. Yes, I knew him before the incident. Anyway, don't be afraid to threaten him. Tell him you will expose his false testimony in your father's case.

Deji's eyes welled with tears.

Threaten him to open case 1163 about the policeman who was sent to kill your dad in prison, of which Tom Holmes burned the documents of proof. Tell him I have copies of these documents, still.

Deji showed the documents on the screen, full and clear, reciting how the police sent someone to kill my father in prison.

If he confiscated whatever device you're using to watch this, tell him that the W has access to the documents and will expose him.

How will they time that? How will they know you threatened him and he didn't abide by the rules?

This video has a signal stamp to it, meaning once it's opened, those five people got notified. The signal works on face recognition, so anyone who has opened it before you doesn't count. Crazy are the technologies we can use these days.

You may ask how Tom Holmes knows about my wife when he is a threat himself? You may ask, how come he doesn't know where Andrew is since he knows my wife? You will understand when you meet her.

He removed the documents and told me his last words:

If I'm dead, try not to hate me. When my wife tells you the truth, you may have a place in your heart to love me, still. But I promise you will meet Andrew and take him into your arms again.

When the video ended, I could hear myself talking to the officer outside the door. I couldn't remember what we said. All I could focus on was getting to Andrew. I took a deep breath and brought myself back to the moment. I gripped the gun in my hands and pointed it at the door.

"I'm pointing my gun at the door, officer," I said. "I will shoot you before you break-in."

"Don't do this—"

"Shut the fuck up and get me Tom Holmes," I demanded.

To my surprise, Tom Holmes spoke, "I'm here, Kate," he said.

I heard him asking the officers to leave the room so he could converse in private with me.

I waited until he spoke again, "I'm alone now. Let me inside."

"Don't try any tricks, Tom. I know about what you've done to Kyle Mason."

Tom said nothing, but I could hear him chew on his gum, so loud and distressed that I knew he was testing me to know how much I knew.

"I know you ditched the papers about the men sent to kill my father in prison."

39

Tom entered, handed me his gun, and sat on the edge of the bathtub before me. Only then did the notion of what happened to my father begin to eat at me from the inside out.

Poor Kyle Mason, who did you piss off so much they did that to you?

Tom asked me what I knew with cold-blooded eyes. I recited Deji's words and then showed him the documents he held up in the video.

Tom sweated inside the crammed bathroom, surprisingly shocked by Deji leaving a recording behind, then stopped chewing his gum.

"Who is Deji's wife," I said.

"You don't know how to shoot this gun, Kate," he said. "Put it down. I'm not going to hurt you."

"Then tell me where I can find Deji's wife."

"I would, only if you realize that you will get her killed."

"Don't play games."

"If you're okay with killing the people who try to help you, be my guest. Adaolisa, Jason, the list goes on."

Talking about Jason felt like a punch to the gut.

"Why didn't they kill me as well?"

"Because you can lead them to Andrew," he said, full of himself, and started chewing again.

"I'm just bait, then?"

"It goes both ways. The world is complicated. They don't want you to dig deep, but also, you could lead them to Andrew. The paradox on interests in life, you can say."

"I'm willing to risk it."

"Okay," he said. "Can I ask you what the black man told you before he died?"

"Are you bargaining with me, Tom Holmes?"

"Why not? You have documents that can put me in jail. As much as you have the upper hand, I don't have much to lose anymore."

"Why does it matter what the black man said? Do you know him?"

"I know he is Najimbian. I know he is from Adaolisa's family, which has been in a centuries-long feud with Deji's family. So, let's say I'm just curious."

"He said *Ouna, Ouna,*" I said. "The same words Deji used to say to his friends as kids when the troops came for them."

"I see. Why do you think he said it?"

"Maybe he was friends with Deji."

"Maybe he was telling you to run."

"It didn't cross my mind, but what difference does it make?"

"Adaolisa and her brother, the man you killed, were Deji's enemies by traditional means in their country's tribal beliefs. They, however, disapproved of what was happening and wanted the killings to stop," he explained. "They were trying to help."

"Does that mean that you know why she sent me the message?"

"I don't know its purpose, but I assume she tried to convince you that you can find your son, which will never happen."

"Lies and lies again. Your words make no sense and lead me to nothing as always."

"Here is what you need to know. Adaolisa and her brother challenged their people and pissed them off. As a result, they killed her instantly."

I didn't mind him giving me all these details. This puzzle looked like it was slowly coming to a resolution.

"How come an African tribe in a small country has the power to execute such crimes in our country?"

"They're a small tribe backed up by big fish and big money — probably from our country."

"If you're telling me the truth, why did her brother kill Jason?"

"Her brother didn't kill Jason. He was protecting the USB."

I had to think it over. Did I kill the man who was trying to help me?

"Who shot Jason, then?"

"Who said he was shot?" Tom said. "He was poisoned by coffee, or latte, or whatever you people drink for comfort these days. Jason was allergic to almond milk, remember? Very few people are allergic to it in the world. One of them was Jason."

Words didn't help now. Memories of Jason never touching his coffee came flooding back. I remember now when he mentioned it the first time we met. I never thought it was that serious, though. Every time we ordered coffee, which was only a few times because he was more into spirits and alcohol, he only touched the glass with the tip of his fingers.

"How come it killed him so fast? How come he never smelled it?"

"Whoever killed him intensified the dose and probably used it with another substance, so his anaphylactic shock would come sooner than later," Tom explained. "These people only need fragments of factual information to make things stick and build a story, then get away with crimes. You see it every day in the news. So and so was charged with killing the man he yelled at in a meeting two days ago, so having a feud with that man is used now to convict him. It's utter nonsense. People love this crap and never use their minds or indisputable logic. It works."

"I assume no one will be held accountable, as the investigation will be called an accident."

"A misfortunate accident," he corrected me. "It happens every day.

Research death allergies in restaurants and fast-food places all over the world. It's a known execution-style they use."

"Who are they?" I asked desperately.

"Don't ask me, Kate," Tom spat his gum out the bathroom's open window. "I don't know who they are."

"Then why do you keep protecting them?"

"I said it before and hate to repeat it. It's my job. They don't tell you that part of being a policeman may entail you breaking the law for the elite when you sign up, but you eventually figure it out."

"Are you trying to sound like a victim now?"

"I'm not. I'm just saying that my wife was pregnant, and I had lung cancer, and the bills are hard to pay. Then I realized what I'd gotten myself into. It wasn't about morals anymore. It was purely Darwinian. He who adapts survives."

"Poetic," I scoffed. "Now, if you don't have anything else you want to tell me, I'd like to know where to find Deji's wife."

"Sure," he laced his hands before him, looking like he was giving up. "Her address is...."

The shock hit me so hard when I heard the address that I lowered my gun. Tom could've quickly cuffed me then and there, but I sensed his sympathy. His regret.

"I know it's hard to take," he said. "but before you go, I need you to hit me with that gun in my face."

"What?"

"I need an explanation of how you jumped out of the window and escaped, stealing my car keys to go wherever you needed to."

"I can't hit you, Tom."

"Really?" He pouted at me.

"I know I killed a man, but I wasn't myself."

"How about you not being yourself again?" he said. "He didn't die yet if it helps. Now, hand me that gun."

"No."

"Hand me the bloody gun, Kate. I'm not going to hurt you. I need a reason to let you escape."

He pulled the gun from my hand and hit himself in the head.

He must've not done this before because he hit himself too hard. He fell on his back in the tub. I froze, watching blood spread around his head.

"Tom? You okay?"

"I should've never stopped smoking," he coughed, looking dizzy. "If I'm going to die, I'd like to die doing what I love."

"I'm sorry you hit yourself," I said absently, thinking about the address of Deji's wife. "And thank you."

"You bloody threatened to send me to jail, Kate," he tried to straighten himself in the tub but failed. "So don't act as if I did you a favor. We do what we have to do so we get through another day. Now jump out the goddamn window. I have to call for the officers to send me to the hospital."

I started to make my way out the window, but before I climbed out, I still asked him, "Why did Deji marry her? Do you know?"

"The best place to hide a secret is in front of everybody's eyes. People look for answers in faraway places when a close-up would've spared time, Kate Mason. Now go find your son."

40

I stood at the entrance of Deji's wife's building and looked at her name on the wall before I pressed the button so she could let me in.

My emotions were in turmoil, mirroring the way I looked with blood on my hands and the silly business outfit. I'd taken off the jacket long ago and stood in my blouse and oversized and absurd business trousers. I knew I looked crazy.

My hands hesitated to push the button because I didn't know how to handle the situation.

Was I going to be aggressive with her? Or was I going to forget her betrayal and beg her to tell me where my son was?

The distant sirens of a police car reminded me of the scant chance I had to find out before they caught me. I forgot all hesitation and I pushed the button.

"Yes?" She answered reasonably fast.

"It's me," I said.

"Kate?" She replied.

"In the flesh."

"Oh, my God. What happened?"

"What do you mean?"

"You're all over the news."

"Why are you acting so surprised?" I had to test her. "You knew something like this would happen eventually, right?"

She took her time to answer. Her breath crackled in the speaker. "I don't know that much, but...."

"I'm here because Deji sent me."

Another round of prolonged silence saturated the air between us. "Are you alone?"

"Why do you ask?"

"Are you alone, Kate?" She tensed.

"I am. Why wouldn't I be?"

"None of us are safe now, that's why," she said. "I didn't want to hurt you. I didn't want to be part of this. I didn't want to lie to you, but Deji insisted — and frankly, I thought he was crazy."

"Enough with the drama. Tell me where my son is."

She buzzed the door open, "Come up. Unfortunately, it's not that black and white."

I entered the building without looking behind me to see if I was being followed. Most of this felt like a dream to me. Lies and revelations that shattered my past life in pieces.

Before her door, I rang the bell, and she opened it.

A tense moment where she didn't have the nerve to invite me in occurred between us. And while I've seen her a million times in my life, I felt like I was staring at someone I hadn't met before. The fact and the body were nothing but a mask that sooner or later had to be taken off.

"Emma," I said, and nothing else.

"Please come in," she ushered me inside.

I entered cautiously, my eyes scanning to inspect her home.

"Don't worry, I'm alone," she said and closed the door.

"How long have you been married to my husband," I faced her. "Is that even legal?"

Emma, looking distressed, seemed to have a serious demeanor about her.

"How about we go there?" She pointed at the balcony.

I cocked my head at her.

I'm not sure if anyone's listening. She mouthed to me.

It took me a moment to comprehend until she pointed at the TV in her living room. My face was everywhere.

A mentally unstable mother kills an innocent African man and escapes a British detective after almost killing him.

"Tom said the African man was still alive," I said in rage.

"Shush," Emma said and pointed at the balcony.

We went to the balcony, and she looked down, checking whether the police were around or not.

"Look," she said. "You and I have very little time."

"So tell me what I need to know."

"The first thing you need to know is that I don't know much. Deji told me to keep a secret one week before the accident," she said. "He begged me to keep a phone number to give you if you needed it after seven years."

"What are you talking about? I don't care about phone numbers. Tell me about this marriage thing. Tell me where my son is."

"I don't know where your son is, but she does," she pulled out a folded yellow note from her pocket with a phone number on it. Under the number, it read, 'Deji's first wife.'

I pulled back, pursing my lips, "I said enough with the games."

She came forward and whispered in my ears, "I'm not her. Deji did that to distract Tom, making him think I was his secret wife and that I knew where Andrew was. They interrogated me repeatedly and then threatened me with videos of people I had sex with in my apartment. But they let me go when they realized I knew nothing."

"You're lying."

"I'm not. Nothing happened between Deji and me. It was a distraction, and Tom and his men never knew what it meant. So here is my question, how did you know about it?"

"Tom told me?"

"Why would he?"

"Jason gave me a USB with a video of Deji telling me to bargain with Tom to tell me."

Emma's face went paler than usual, "My God. So this means Tom told you only to find out what was going on. I'm sure that he never truly believed me to be who Deji called his wife. Deji visited me every week three months before the train incident to give them the impression that he was cheating on you, and they swallowed the bait."

"What are you talking about?"

"They will kill me, like Jason and the others."

"Emma," I gritted my teeth. "What are you talking about?"

She tensed and grabbed me, "Look, I love you, and I never thought Deji was telling the truth. I can't believe this is happening, but Kate, get out of this house and call this number. It's Deji's wife. She knows everything. I'm the messenger, that's all."

"If what you're saying is true, and Tom played me, we're ambushed already."

"No, because he can't touch you before discovering who the real Deji's wife is. Had it been me, he'd want to know if I knew where Andrew is. It's complicated, but she can explain it to you."

"So you're suggesting I call his wife and meet her? Won't they kill us both?"

"I have an idea," she whispered again, pointing inside her living room. "I'm pretty sure no one hears me on the balcony because I've checked it repeatedly. This guy I dated who worked in surveillance and helped me with it. He even told me he found nothing in my apartment. Still, he told me about the government using something called 'Pegasus II,' which can read text messages, track calls, collect passwords, location tracking, and access the target device's microphone. All through the phone. You don't even have to open a file. All they do is send you a signal, and you're caught in their web of surveillance technology."

"That's why you kept your phone inside," I said. "Where is this going, Emma?"

"You and I enter the apartment and fake this conversation again," she said. "I'll give you a fake number and tell you to go call it, so they follow a wrong lead."

I took a moment to admire her cunningness. "Just like in movies, huh."

"Movies are entertaining; this is scary," she said. "Let's do it. We have no time."

"Where are you going to get a fake number? We can't use one that isn't real, or they will figure it out."

"Don't worry; I'll use one of my one-night-stands."

"You're kidding me. I don't want to do wrong to anyone whose innocent."

"Son of Senator Kane, innocent?" She scoffed. "Trust me, I should've 'me too'd' him, but I didn't dare speak."

41

Emma's plan worked. She lent me some cash and a change of clothes. A headscarf and large fancy glasses helped my not-so-professional disguise.

Once I left the building, I took a regular taxi since I decided not to own a phone after Emma told me about the surveillance.

I pretended I was lost in London in the taxi and told the driver to cruise for a while. I secretly wanted to know if I was being followed. He mumbled his objections but began praising the Lord for customers like me when I slid him enough money.

When I saw that I probably wasn't being followed, I offered him more money if he allowed me to make a call from his phone. I told him my battery had died.

His smile broadened, and he said in an Indian accent, "*Secrets boyfriend, ooh? Not first time I see this. I know everything.*"

He handed me his phone, and I dialed Deji's wife's number, not trying to speculate on her identity. I assumed that I didn't know her. Not out of optimism, but because there was no one else left in my life who didn't betray me.

She didn't pick up.

I wasn't surprised, so I sent her a message. I wanted to let her know that Deji sent me and cut to the chase:

Deji's wife to Deji's wife.

I'm Kate.

He told me to call you.

You know where Andrew is.

Emma gave me the number.

The reply came fast. A little too fast, it almost worried me.

Piccadilly Square. I'll find you.

Then I had to add:

I'm wearing oversized glasses and a headscarf.

***

I circled in Piccadilly Square, and I wondered if I should've been more cautious. The space here was too open for an easy target. But then I remembered Tom Holmes's idea about hiding in front of everyone's eyes.

I adjusted my scarf and glasses and calmed myself, speculating how this Runaway Train worked.

I ran over all the details and events in my mind. The best I could come up with was that the terrorist attack was a staged play. The hooded terrorists stopped the train and spoke long enough for the passengers to confirm their language later. Then they picked up their targets, making everyone think they were victims.

It sounded like a brilliant plan to me. Had the Runaway Train been a commercial transportation, I'd have booked first class many years ago and started my life all over.

I imagined, however, another passenger on the train saw the so-called terrorists with their own eyes. No one could've doubted the kidnapped passengers were part of the plan. It all fit the W's theory to protect those who needed an escape and a new identity. The only downside, in my opinion, was the trauma and fear they bestowed on the other passengers.

Like Katherine told me, nothing was black and white, and everyone eventually was in it for themselves.

One of the things that always puzzled me about the attack was that no one got hurt. But, of course, in retrospect, I knew it was intentional because this wasn't an actual attack.

Not that I fully comprehended it all, but why ask for a British prisoner in exchange? I understood they did that to complete their masterful play, but did Deji have a terrorist brother? If so, how did they know the government wouldn't reciprocate?

"When you turn around, don't panic," the voice said behind me. "Act as if we're friends and hug me."

I turned around and saw a black woman, wearing a scarf and glasses like me, except that her scarf was green and yellow, colors to compliment her beautiful dark skin.

I played along, saying something like "hey' without mentioning names, and hugged her.

"Always late, Samira!" She called me, pointing at her watch, sounding obnoxiously loud.

Her accent was inescapable. Najimbian like Deji's. I realized why she asked me not to panic when she took her glasses off.

I recognized her.

42

I stared at Lupita, the woman from the theatre whom Deji claimed was stalking him.

"Let's go for a walk," she said as she put her glasses back on.

I walked along in silence, wanting to ask any questions. Somehow her being Deji's wife didn't hurt me. Before my time, they must've married years earlier, probably under Najimbian laws.

"Get rid of the number you called me from," she said.

"I borrowed the taxi driver's number. Unfortunately, I don't have one now."

"Smart girl. I left mine in the limo parked by the curb behind me. Don't look. If shit hits the fan, like you Americans say, run to it. The driver knows what to do next."

"Oh," I resisted looking back.

"Smile while you're listening to me in our walk," she said. "Please don't ask too many questions until I unload my misery onto you."

Her English was much better than Deji's. I was all ears.

"I married Deji when we were fifteen in Najimbia. We're the same age. He wasn't the love of my life, but I liked him a lot."

"Okay?"

"We didn't marry because we wanted to. We married because of the law."

"Law?"

"You call it tradition where you're from. To us, it's the law. It can't be broken. The day I was born, I was spoken for. My marital life was planned when I hadn't become a woman yet. I abided by the rules. The penalty was exile, sometimes death."

"Okay?"

"Whom I really loved was Deji's brother, Kejani Olanti."

"The terrorist?" I couldn't stop myself from offending her.

"Don't worry. He was a terrorist. At least he turned into one. I didn't know then. He deserves what happened to him."

"What happened to him?"

"The authorities tortured him to death at some point and bribed another prisoner to kill him."

"Like my father?"

"Like your father," she speculated. "I don't know much about his story."

"I didn't think you would. Tell more about Kejani's death."

"His existence made the British authorities think of me as the terrorist's mistress. It was the reason they contacted Katherine to hypnotize Deji in case he was growing up to become another terrorist like his brother."

"Thank you for answering the question my mother wouldn't." I offered with gratitude.

"All of this is just a background story for why your son was taken," she squeezed my hand while looking ahead. "I need you to be patient, so you get the whole picture. It's a bit of a long story."

I nodded, trying not to get emotional.

"Hey, look!" She faked being cheery all of a sudden, pointing at whatever she found exciting behind me. "I have to take a photo of you here."

I played along and stood helpless as she took the photo.

"Perfect, I did that because of some pedestrian looking at us. I don't know who is who anymore," she said, and then we walked side by side again. "To make you understand the bigger picture, I need to tell you about two families from Najimbia."

"The Olanti and Igbo."

"Yes," she nodded. "I'm not sure if you as a westerner will believe what I'm about to tell you."

"Trust me. I've learned to believe the unbelievable by now."

"Good," she took a deep breath. "Centuries ago, an Olanti found his wife cheating on him with a man from the Igbo. He shot him in the head and buried her alive."

I said nothing, alarmed by the morbid story that was unfolding.

"Sounds like an old-fashioned tale that most people would not think can happen these days. People think that we as a species have advanced and have been civilized. So far from it," she sighed. "Anyway, the Igbo decided they have to kill a member of an Olanti in response."

"Brutal."

"Wait until you see brutal," she said. "The Olanti had one of their own killed by the Igbo, and also in response, they decided to kill one of the Igbo back."

"I'm sensing it never stopped?"

"Not only did it not stop, but it escalated."

"What do you mean?"

"Fifty years later, having lived through a member of each family being killed every few weeks, the Olanti created a committee to look into the matter. When I say committee, I'm talking about a rural bunch of older men who are barely educated beyond the ancient beliefs of their fathers. Beliefs that permit them to bury women and children and chop off men's heads for opposition ideologies. The Igbo were not different, by the way."

"I think I've heard stories about this."

"You haven't heard shit," she said but wasn't tense about it. She came across as the strong woman I'd like to be. "The committee, instead of backing off or forgiving the Igbo, or offering religious sacrifice, decided the only way to feel better about themselves was to kill the Igbo's most loved man."

"Man?"

"Women were, and still are, out of the equation because women aren't superior beings according to the two tribes. Killing them is of no value or price to make the tribe proud."

"Awful."

"The Olanti started a fire that could never be put out. First, they targeted the most loved man in the tribe. When they were asked to describe what a most loved man meant, they said, '*he whom his mother will cry her heart out and slit her wrists in mourning.*'"

"You're scaring me," I had to face her.

"Don't look at me. Everyone around us should think we're two women on a casual walk with no worries," Lupita said. "Collect yourself if you want to help your son. Now go buy us some ice cream, and calm down. One for me, and one for you."

I did as she said, Reluctantly, realizing it was too cold for ice cream. Probably she suspected someone else was curious about us.

I bought the ice cream, feeling her pain but admiring her not getting emotional about it. Then, we continued our walk around Piccadilly Square.

"The Igbo's most loved man died, and they decided to hit back," she said. "This time, they didn't go for the most loved man in the Olanti, but the *youngest*, most loved. In their words, '*the one whose mother will mourn the most and will curse God for taking his life at such a young age, just when he was about to experience this blooming life.*'"

"You sound like they had these sentences written in a book or something. I mean like code."

"It was. Each of the tribes had a testament of sorts. A dark testament that changed according to the killing through the years."

"What about religion?"

"Religion was considered a domestic matter in the tribes. It didn't affect their so-called foreign policies. The Olanti were Muslims. The Igbo were Christians. This may have ignited the situation, but none of their religious elders had a say in the matter. It's tribal, territorial, and animalistic. Born out of ignorance, poverty, and brainwashed ideologies. It meant more to each tribe than anyone could've imagined. It meant bonding over their rival's tragedy. It meant their leaders ruled with a strong grip by creating an enemy. It meant they had holidays celebrating victory, which was the killing of the other's tribes' most important men. It meant justice."

"All because one man had his woman cheat on him centuries ago?"

"Do you think enemies still remember why they hate each other? The reason that started it all goes unremembered with time. What's left is souls with black goo spurting out darkness onto each other."

"I don't think I will ever understand. What about the Najimbian government?"

"They didn't have a say either. For one, the government members were either Olanti or Igbo, so it was an inside job. As for those rational people in the government who wanted to stop it, they were executed most of the time, ironically enough in collaboration between the two tribes."

"Are you telling me the two tribes wanted it to go on?"

"It's hard to answer this. Evil seeps through the blood from generation to generation and common sense and humanity freeze in the background. Those in either tribe who wanted to oppose their own because they didn't support this endless revenge killing story were also exiled or killed."

"Like Adaolisa Igbo, I suppose."

"And her brother," she said. "They helped the W with the Runaway Train because they believed in the cause. Adaolisa later sent you the message, realizing that only you at the wedding didn't have a hidden agenda. Her brother watched Jason about to give you the USB and supported the idea but then witnessed him die, which urged him to keep the USB and give it to you."

"Why didn't he stop when I chased him, then?"

"Because you were about to expose him, and thus he was going to get killed by his people," she said. "Adaolisa was the same. What do you think stopped her from meeting you and telling you in the face? Sending you the message was her way of giving you a clue. I'll tell you more about what she expected of you later. Had Emma's fiancé not pointed her out while watching you from behind the bushes, she wouldn't have had to run. She watched to see what you were going to do about it."

"Why then?" I had to ask. "Why send me the message on my wedding day?"

For the first time, Lupita looked back at me with sympathy. Then, she nodded, "There is a perfect explanation for that."

"Did Deji send her?"

"No."

"Then who wanted to stop me from marrying Jason?"

"Me."

"You?" I asked with disbelief. "Why?"

"Because, even though I'm still legally Deji's wife under Najim-bian laws, I knew he wouldn't like it. It killed him being unable to give you your son back, and I couldn't watch you marry another man who wasn't fully honest with you."

"I don't believe you, Lupita," I said, unsure why I didn't. I didn't feel like Deji had the right to control my life while not telling me what was happening to my son. I loved them, and deep inside, I didn't think he would do what Lupita made Adaolisa do.

Lupita took off her glasses and sighed, "Okay, I lied."

"You're making it hard for me to trust you now."

"I don't think so. Everything I told you and am about to tell you is true. I was trying to protect the person who told me to tell Adaolisa to send you the message."

"Don't tell me it's...."

"I need you to stay calm and not ask me about him until the end so I can tell you all you needed to know in detail for the last eight years."

"It was Andrew, right?"

"He risked his life contacting me, but yes, he couldn't stand watching you marry another man, not knowing what happened," she said solemnly. "Now, let me continue the story about the Olanti and Igbo's eternal feud."

43

Sensing my emotional dilemma, Lupita decided to buy two umbrellas that we could hide beneath. My eyes scanned our surroundings as I felt her suspicion that we were being watched. Craning my neck up, I wondered if someone was watching from the roofs of the buildings that surrounded us. That would have been an easy shot.

It began to rain as if higher powers offered assistance and sheltered us from our enemies with the blanket of the sudden downpour. I needed to believe in a higher power that Deji and Emma always talked about in my darkest hour.

Still, it wasn't clear to me who my enemy was. The police? Was it the people Tom Holmes talked about? The Olanti? The Igbo? It also occurred to me that Emma did her best to help. I hope she didn't get in trouble. I didn't want her blood on my hands too. Did Tom Holmes follow the long trail of the number I messaged?

Emma had sent her Senator's son boyfriend a vague message: *I need to see you about that thing I wanted to tell you. I'm bringing a sexy friend over.*

I didn't know the details of her relationship with that man she hated but wasn't surprised when he told her to come over.

The plan was for Emma to stall in the house and then send him another message that she and her friend, me, had to be an hour late. This way, she bought me precious time, and hopefully, Tom's men didn't recognize me leaving the apartment in my disguise.

"Here," she handed me an umbrella. "The rain will help. It'll make it harder for anyone to find us."

"Who are we afraid of exactly?"

"There are many to be afraid of, but let me continue," she said. "For two hundred years, the feudal revenge story continued. Let me also remind you that this isn't just a Najimbian thing. I know at least three other countries where this has been happening for centuries."

"Why is this never mentioned in the news?"

"Oh, Western news happily claim there are weapons of mass destruction in these countries, but never the existence of people and ideologies of mass destruction," she scoffed, "Why? So many reasons. The West has common interests with the Olanti and the Igbo, concerning oil and gas and natural resources."

"I heard this too many times by now. Is that it?"

"Also, the Olanti and the Igbo have mercenaries who happily do dirty work for the West. Disposable poor human beings who'll die either way, family feuds or dirty black ops. All the dirty money laundered through Najimbia is also presented as charity work and helping the poor. If they really sent money to countries like us, why do you think we never changed?"

"I guess what you're really saying is that no one really cares," I said. "I'd be lying if I told you I cared because I only cared after what happened to my son."

"The insane war of killing went on and on. Beloved victims, youngest and richest from either tribe. Both tribes continued to find a way to intensify the pain for the other tribe's families, which caused feudal rivalry within the tribes. A young brother whose turn never came to die because he was considered a lesser, not so valuable person was hated by his older one who worked hard and knew that aspiring to be a better human being was his ticket for his demise."

"It's bonkers thinking this is real life, not a fantasy."

"At some point, rules were set between the tribes," Lupita said. "They agreed on a list beforehand, instead of randomly choosing every time."

"A list? Are you serious?"

"Dead serious. For example, using British names, Harry Olanti, a renowned doctor, is announced as the Igbo's next kill. Harry could've been working all his life as hard as possible and now has a family. Once his name is out, he's fucked. Moreover, Harry can't escape or even attempt to appeal because that will prompt them just to kill his family," she shook her head, unable to fathom something she'd been trying to understand for years. "Now listen to this: if Harry escaped and the Igbo killed his family because of his cowardice, the dead family doesn't count as a kill."

"Meaning?"

"Meaning the Olanti still owed the Igbo one of their own. It was the only punishment for Harry's escape."

"Why would both tribes agree to this mess?"

"I never knew, though I've always questioned it. Their eyes have been wooled by years of hate and repetition. Deji once told me about men imprisoned and tortured for years without human connection or even being intimate with a woman. Of course, when they were released, they would hire a hooker to satisfy their primal urges, but when it came down to doing the deed, the traumatized men couldn't even touch them. They could only masturbate in front of them because they no longer knew how to use physical connection or intimacy. They had endured brutality for years, and it disconnected them from human connection, even though they wanted to on some deeper level."

"And the same goes with the feud," I realized. "Years of hatred turned into a monotonous crime no one rose an eyebrow at. Didn't anyone ever try to interfere and talk reason?"

"They were killed. I told you so already. Now, let's go to the limo," she said, already walking in its direction, and I followed her, "Let's talk about the part that concerns Deji."

44

I sat in the backseat beside her, closed my eyes, and exhaled, "I understand now."

"What do you understand, Kate?" She signaled for the silent African driver to drive.

"Deji's mother smuggled him over to the UK, leaving the girls behind. No one would come after the girls, but probably his time would come, offered by his tribe and taken by the enemy."

"True, you understand. He didn't kill her, by the way. She died defending him from his people. The Olanti, was about to kill him in his escape for not being man enough and dying according to tradition if his time came."

"Was it Deji's time then?"

"It was his brother's," she said. "But Kejani escaped with me to the UK earlier. I cheated on Deji with his cool, rebellious brother, knowing the Najimbian marriage laws didn't apply in the UK."

I saw her stop with her melted ice cream and fidget. Her hands trembled, and she dropped the cone in the garbage can in the center console between us. I did the same, and I realized I had melted ice cream on my hands, not having tasted it. Let alone remember I was holding it.

"Anyway," Lupita continued. "Kejani Olanti wasn't a terrorist then. He was wild and dangerous but not a terrorist. He had an aspiring career as a short distance runner."

"Both brothers were athletic then."

"We immigrants have a complex relationship with past and present. The idea of capitalism and the West doing unjust to our kind wrapped his mind in a carcass of nihilism. Spice it up with drugs, women, and bad company, and you've got yourself a fresh young terrorist."

"What does this have to do with Deji?"

"Deji hardly contacted his brother, knowing he took a darker path in life."

"I imagine he also didn't want to see you with him."

"You imagined right. As much as Kejani turned into a beast, his original trauma was based on him being announced as Igbo's next kill."

I had to think this over, then said, "Why would the Igbo's next kill be someone like Kejani who, don't take it the wrong way, doesn't strike as of value?"

"Because Kejani had won an international runner's game at the world cup in Switzerland for under eighteen years once."

"I see."

"For the Olanti to see their own youngster's face on every news channel holding the cup and wearing the Najimbian flag, then thanking his tribe, was worth life, death, and beyond."

"I assume Kejani becoming a terrorist and killing the British senator made him unworthy of the next kill," I couldn't believe I just said that.

"Yes," she stopped without looking my way.

"And the rules demanded his family killed, so it was Deji's time," I stopped.

Lupita turned around, her face unclear and challenging to read. Her blank expression resembled a ghost from a distant parallel world that had nothing to do with the reality I thought I was part of. Her blurred face scared me, even though she didn't intend to do so. It scared me because I was afraid of what she would say next.

"It wasn't Deji's time, Kate," she resigned.

"But, if I understand the rules, it should've been, right?" I questioned with hesitation. Again, my mind resisted the harsh truth, trying to bargain and argue with reality. My voice didn't sound like my own when I had finally gathered my thoughts. "If I understood correctly, the next valuable person whose mother will slit her wrist knowing of his death should be Deji—"

"Take a deep breath, Kate," Lupita said sympathetically. "You're crying."

I didn't know I had let my emotions rule the moment. I could barely grasp my swirling thoughts, let alone hold back any feelings that came with them. I didn't want to admit that I'd sobbed each syllable in the last sentence.

"Whose turn was it, Lupita?" I cried with desperation.

"The one who was most valuable in their eyes, Kate," she said. "I'm sorry. He didn't do anything wrong. He just fit the bill. The younger, the most valuable to his parent who now lives abroad, and the one who'll become a British citizen. In their eyes, that was valuable."

"And the one was born an Olanti," I sobbed.

"It was Andrew's turn," she said quietly. "That's why Deji got him on the Runaway Train. He had to disappear from the face of the earth, or the Igbo would've killed him. Had you been in contact with him, the Olanti themselves would have killed you because you were not of their blood."

She let me cry for a little longer, knowing I needed to finally let out all the pain, confusion, and distress, along with the shock of finally knowing why Andrew was taken from me.

"Tell me more," I raised my head after a while.

"For the past seven years, there was no way to find him. However, now that the government declared him and Deji dead, they should forget about him," she explained. "Still, now and then, something could happen, rules can change, old kills that failed could be resurrected. You never know."

"So, how do I find my son?" I gritted my teeth. "And don't you dare warn me about getting killed. I'm dead already."

"There is only one way," she said. "It's a sacrifice. A tribal one that a few men dare to perform."

"Will it get my son back?"

"I'm not sure, but you said you'd do anything. And given that you're a fugitive here right now, I think it's the only way."

"Okay," I held back the tears and wiped my eyes, ready for the impossible. "You said it's a sacrifice performed by men? Can't I perform it?"

"It's never been done," Lupita said. "No woman has ever offered to do it before."

"I'll give it a shot. Tell me what to do. Who do I have to meet? Where do I have to go?"

"I've already made contact," she sighed, pointing at the street ahead of where we're heading. "I had a hunch you wouldn't give up. Well, Deji said exactly that - you wouldn't give up."

"Are we going where I think we're going?"

"Yes. You'll get a chance to meet with the Igbo's leader and ask him to forgive your son and let him live."

"I don't understand," I responded, feeling more confused than confident.

"If you're asking how you will meet with him, I'll explain soon. The point is that you have to treat him like a God to spare your son."

"I will do whatever it takes," I said, watching the limo stop by our destination's entrance.

Lupita held my hand again and said, "Remember when I told you about the rules the two tribes made?"

"Of course."

"One of the rules is more of an exception than a rule. It's hardly ever used, but you might be able to pull it off."

"What rule is that?"

"An eye for an eye," Lupita said. "A mother for the son."

Never mind that I still couldn't understand this new underworld I was dealing with, but if that was the solution to save Andrew, I was all in. Lupita probably never had children and didn't understand what I'd do for Andrew as his mother. She didn't understand that logic had nothing to do with sacrificing myself for him. She didn't know that the pain of death would be a reverie of the life I'd give him. This undeniable truth only came with being a parent, and I would give my life for his in the blink of an eye, even after all these years.

I nodded in agreement, and she nodded back as we felt the car stop. The driver finally came around and opened the door for us to enter the W.

45

The W's building was creepy and unsettling.

All walls were white from the inside, sterile and uninviting, and very few people worked at the reception. They were to guide Lupita and me to wherever we needed to go. Every corridor was blocked with a white door that needed a magnetic keycard. It seemed abandoned, but I understood that every department was isolated from the other.

I saw a couple of men in suits that looked like Jason. I finally understood his struggle to learn more about the W's secrets. Everyone kept to themselves and wasn't supposed to know about the other floors or departments.

Lupita didn't talk but signed a paper at the reception desk. The receptionist was dressed overly professional for her role, and she told us to follow her. At first, I thought we were following her to a wall, but it chugged open, and we rode the elevator.

It was hard to tell how many floors we rode up because that white box of mystery didn't feel like we were even moving. The door finally opened again to yet another white room.

"You're sure you want to do this?" Lupita asked one last time, looking at me with such serious eyes.

"I have no doubts," I reassured her with conviction.

"Okay, so here is the deal. You will be meeting with the Igbo tribal king; they call him the monarchy. His name is Exuma Azanu. You never address him with anything but Manocho, which is translated to my master or my lord."

"Okay," I replied, taking it all in.

"When you talk to him, you bow your head. You don't look in his eyes, and you don't offend him."

"Fair enough."

"Never before has a woman asked to spare her son because women are...."

"...not a superior being to them, I understand."

"And because of that, you will be treated as a man in preparation."

"Preparation?" I asked with a bit of confusion.

"This is ritual. Manocho is a God to his tribe. It's a holy event. So, yes, there are preparations."

"I'm ready," I said. "Is that all?"

"Mostly."

"I have questions before the preparation. Is Exuma—"

"Manocho, I said." Lupita quickly corrected.

"I'm sorry. Manocho, is he here in the building?"

"No. He's in Najimbia. You will meet him on a zoom call," Lupita said. "Believe me. It took years to persuade him to show up and use such technology. To him, seeing someone through a screen in a faraway county is almost witchcraft."

I wasn't going to comment, but I wanted to, for I could have said a lot on this matter. One of the things that bothered Deji was how some westerners still thought of his people as ignorant and only followed the ancient superstitions. When in fact, many of his people had gone a long way in life to rise above and become doctors, lawyers, physicists, and much more. It was just that the few like Manocho, who still hung onto the past, stained his fellow citizens with such stigma.

"More questions?" Lupita asked, sensing my silence had to be me pondering.

"Of course," I said. "If the W assists people like Deji in escaping their past, how come I'm meeting the tribe that still wants him dead here?"

"Good question. A deal was made between the Igbo and the W. It's politics and money, of course. Being enemies doesn't mean they didn't communicate. It's how things work."

"What incentive does the Igbo have by meeting me?"

"The Manocho wants to know where Andrew is to kill him and prove superiority and strength to his people. Since the W will never tell him, he wants to see you if you're worthy of replacing him and if his people would feel satisfied by your death."

"If they do, how will I get killed?"

"Don't worry about that," she scoffed. "They'll find you."

"What guarantees my son lives?"

"You're son is alive with the W's help. They will never tell you where he is because you'll be followed, and he will get killed. You're not here to meet your son. You're here to once and for all keep him alive if the Igbo accepts your sacrifice."

I said nothing, wondering what century I lived in now, for this made it seem like I had been taken back in time. Then again, I was deep enough into the rabbit hole that any attempt of trying to make sense of all these things was futile and absurd.

"I'm ready for the preparation then," I said, focusing only on Andrew's face.

"Then enter this room and take your clothes off," she said.

"What?"

"You're a man now, Kate, and men only present themselves to Manocho in naked form when asking for sacrifice."

46

The white room I entered led to a bathroom. A voice appeared from the speakers and began to speak.

"Please take off your clothes, Mrs. Mason," it had an accent like Deji, but much heavier, not to mention the dialect was a bit different.

"It's Kate."

"Manocho doesn't address women by their names," the voice said.

I resisted rolling my eyes as I took off my clothes, "Then it's Mrs. Olanti."

"Manocho doesn't consider you an Olanti," the voice said flatly. "The Olanti blood doesn't run in your veins."

I said nothing and stood bare naked, waiting for further instructions. Somehow, I didn't feel ashamed or worried. It felt strangely cathartic and liberating, facing my potential death the same way I came in the world, stark naked.

"Please step into the bathroom and turn on the water, Mrs. Mason."

The bathroom had only a wall-long mirror and a small shower. All white. I turned it on and let the water run down my body and cleanse my soul.

"Now, you will need to clap your hands against the wall," the voice said.

"What?"

"It's the cleansing ritual. Please do as I say to meet the Manocho."

I trembled as I followed the instructions as I remembered how Deji locked himself in the bathroom and splashed his hands against the wall. It was surreal to be doing the same, just now.

"Please repeat after me," the voice said. "Ouna Ouna."

I felt my heart pounding, and it seemed to nearly burst out of my chest. Was Deji performing a ritual all this time?

"Please say the words, Mrs. Mason. I'm aware you know them well."

I said the words repeatedly as he instructed while splashing my hands against the wall.

"Why would saying 'run, run' be part of this ritual?" I forced myself to ask the male voice. I felt as if I deserved an answer to that question, at least.

"Ouna, Ouna, is not run, run," it said. "It's a phrase that is said when someone asks to spare someone they love by being killed instead."

"Fuck me," I whispered. The wave of realization of all those years I questioned Deji in his showers hit me hard, almost drowning me in emotion.

"No blasphemy, please, Mrs. Mason. This ritual is sacred."

I was spiraling down into and bottomless pit of nightmares. The unending layers of this dystopia could never be navigated back to anything normal again. Nothing could bring me back to the world I thought I knew just a few days ago.

"How long am I supposed to do that?"

"Until your soul is cleansed, Mrs. Mason."

"How will I know when my soul is cleansed?" I began to cry again, sobbing slowly, unable to take the pressure and face the madness. The water splashing over my face, my body, carried my tears with it down the drain.

"It's being cleansed now, Mrs. Mason. The tears are your redemption."

There was no point in talking anymore, not even resisting. I fully allowed myself to let go of every pain, every betrayal, every trauma, and every loss. The tears flowed freely and swiftly as I continued to slap my hands against the shower wall.

Eventually, the slaps became easier to do, and the tears began to dry up. I had lost all sense of time, but I could feel myself becoming lighter. My words became more coherent. My breathing began to feel calmer. I barely had the strength to carry on with the ritual when I heard the voice again.

All I naively wished was that Deji stood outside that bathroom door, waiting to comfort me like I used to do with him.

"May the Gods bless you, Mrs. Mason," the voice said, "Now, please go to the mirror and pick up the white cloth on the side table."

I did as I was instructed, looking at my naked body past the steam created by the long shower I was in.

"Please wrap it around your torso and under your shoulders," the voice said. "It'll cover the rest of your body but show your legs."

As I began to dress, I could only remember Deji wearing the same white clothes in the video. He tried to sacrifice himself a day before the Runaway Train, then realized he failed and had to take Andrew away.

"What you're wearing are simply clothes for modesty," the voice said. "Now the other white folded piece on your left side, this is what's truly of importance."

I turned to look and got chills on my arms. My body seemed to know what my mind had yet to catch on to.

"This, Mrs. Mason, is your shroud," the voice said. "You turn both your palms upward and place it on top."

I did as I was asked in a solemn, silent way.

"Walk with it to the next room where you will meet the Manocho. You'll shortly be in his holy's presence, holding your own shroud in your hands as a sacrifice. May he accept your death instead of your son's, then you will be killed once you leave the W."

47

The next room was all-white as well. All empty except for the wall-sized screen directly in front of me. While holding my shroud as instructed, the image of the Manocho suddenly appeared on the monitor. It made me want to retreat.

Not because he looked evil or like a villain from cliched movies or because I didn't like how he stared at me. What scared me the most was that he looked ordinary.

You couldn't tell he was a man killing families and hunting them for life based on his seemingly normal appearance. He just followed an ingrained belief inside him and looked like he never entertained the idea that he was doing anything wrong.

"You are Mrs. Mason?" He said as he sat in a simple office behind an old wooden desk. Just beyond him, a colorful inlaid glass blocked the scorching sun outside. On his right side stood a noisy fan while two other men sat on the left.

He didn't sit upon a throne, and he wore an old brown suit over a buttoned blue shirt. He cocked his head to the left, taking a better look at me though his grainy camera.

"I am, Manocho," I lowered my head with my shroud in my hands, not sure what I was about to say next.

"*I not approve of meeting like this,*" he said with a thick accent of broken English. "*Welcome Home is bad people. They interfere in other culture. Not good.*"

"I truly apologize," I was forced to play along, but didn't know what else to say in response.

"*No apologize,*" he said. "*Justice will serve. No man stop justice.*"

I closed my eyes, resisting the urge to explain, and counter his argument. We were two different people that not only came from different worlds but almost different ages.

I've always loved Najimbian people who worked with Deji. They were fun and laughed all the time. They were pure at heart and meant good. In fact, they treated women much better than western men and worshipped family. They didn't aspire to be rich. They only wanted to have a place to sleep and enough money to eat.

Still, a few of them, like Manocho, darkened that beautiful image.

"I'm here to present this shroud as a sacrifice," I opened my eyes. "If your holiness approves, I'd wish you take me and forever spare my son."

The Manocho laughed and looked at his men. They also chuckled and shook their heads, following his lead.

"*You not Olanti, Mrs. Mason,*" he said. "*Why I need you?*"

"You don't need me. I need my son. I beg you to leave him be."

"*I see,*" he pursed his lips and said nothing else.

"I know that I'm ignorant of the culture and well aware of how women aren't of value, but I'd do anything for you to spare him."

"*We value woman,*" he said. "*Not in death. Woman make bread. Make children. Make life. Woman is goddess. Death is for men. Life is for woman.*"

I wasn't articulate enough to know what to say to that logic, so I kept my silence, wishing he could guide this conversation.

"*How long you no see Andu?*"

"Andu?"

He seemed puzzled at my questions, looking at his assistants for help. One of them reminded him of my son's actual name.

"Ah, you mean Andrew," I said.

"*No. Andu,*" he insisted, almost offended. "*Androuh is western name, not Olanti. Our son is Andu.*"

I wanted to argue that he was my son, not theirs, the Olanti, but it wasn't going to help my case, "I haven't seen my son for eight years, your holiness."

"*You not know him?*"

"I knew him until he was six."

"*Then you not know him, Mason,*" he insisted, sounding a little angrier.

Calling me Mason didn't bother me, as long as I understood him. I needed him to understand me, to take me in place of Andrew.

"*Why sacrifice for son you not know?*" He asked with suspicion.

"He is my son," I pleaded. "It doesn't matter if I haven't seen him in years."

"*It matter, Mason. He bad man, maybe.*"

What could I have said to that? "Even if he is, I'd like him to live without being hunted by the Igbo. I want him to feel safe."

"*He escape fate, Mason. He die. Today, tomorrow, ten years. Justice. If not, his children die. Eye for eye.*"

"What do I have to do to make you think otherwise?" I begged. "Is there anything that a woman like me can offer you to set him free?"

"*Yes,*" he said, fully serious, no bullshit, no anger. "*Bring him to me. Or kill him.*"

Miraculously I didn't cry or scream or tell him to fuck off. I prayed to a God I didn't believe in that he'd guide me to how to deal with this man. Then I watched him debating with his men in their language.

I resorted to silence, praying their argument had a resolution for me. What else could I offer more than my life to save my son?

"*My men appreciate courage, Mason,*" he finally spoke. "*No woman sacrifice for son before.*"

"I appreciate them appreciating me," I bowed my head at them.

"*Deji ask to sacrifice for son before.*"

"I assumed so. Thank you for telling me."

"*Deji is man. Better sacrifice,*" he said. "*But people,*" he rapped at his chest. "*Not want Deji. People want Andu.*"

"I see."

"*Deji and Andu take Runaway Train,*" he pointed at the W's logo on the wall behind me. "*Bad people make escape. No justice.*"

"I'm sorry," I repeated myself.

"*Question,*" he leaned forward.

"Please ask. I will answer."

"*Deji and Andu leave you,*" he said. "*Why sacrifice?*"

It was a horribly sounding question, especially when I thought of Deji sometimes. I knew he had to, but I still felt like he could've done better. The problem with the Manocho's question wasn't this part, though. It was him not understanding what my family meant to me, whether I liked their choices or not.

I simply replied with the only truth that mattered, "*I love Deji and Andu.*"

"*Love, good,*" he leaned back, stretching the one-syllable word, almost romanticizing it and pointing at his heart. "*I know.*"

"You do?"

"*I love people. I love wife. I love children,*" he said.

"Okay. It seems we share this part."

"*But also love justice,*" he said. "*Look, Mason. My men respect woman like you. You not woman. You man. Brave.*"

I did my best not to crumble in tears like I'd been doing for the past twenty-four hours.

"*We do deal with you.*"

My eyes widened, and my heart skipped a beat. Did I persuade him? Did I do it? I thought it was impossible.

"*We no kill you,*" he said.

"Yes. I mean, thank you, but Andu—"

"*I finish,*" he rapped his hand on the desk.

"I'm sorry, Manocho."

"*You go home. You live. We talk to police in UK. We have deal with UK. Money. Big money. Oil. Secrets. Power. We help. UK help.*"

"And?" I asked fearfully. I didn't like where this was going.

"*You no jail. You free. You no sacrifice.*"

"What about Andu?"

He stopped and talked to his people in their native tongue again. It was apparent that he spoke of me because I could hear the name Mason over and over again.

He returned to face me and said the most absurd thing I've ever heard, "Your last name Mason?"

"Yes, your holiness," I bowed my head. "That's my family name."

"*Your family bad people.*"

"Bad?" I fidgeted. I certainly didn't want him to think that. Was he talking about Katherine? But no, he was talking about the Masons. "No, Manocho. We're good. We love people. We don't hurt anyone."

"You lie," he pointed a finger at the screen. "*You Mason. Freemason.*"

"No," I gasped. "No. No. No. Please don't misunderstand."

"*You make Deji love you, so you take Andu for Freemason,*" his eyes scared me all of a sudden.

I took a step back, really worried, without knowing how to counter this melancholic argument. All I could remember was the memory of Deji, Andrew, and I playing on the floor of my apartment with the Runaway Train. I guess this was going to be my solace for the rest of my life.

"*Andu die when time come,*" he finally announced. "*He on Runaway Train. He with bad Welcome Home. He survive. Escape. We find him. We don't find him. God find him.*"

I was about to get on my knees and beg him, but he'd disconnected the video call before I ever had the chance. My knees still gave in, and I sank to the floor, my shroud sliding from between my hands. After all I'd done, I ended up facing this darkened fate.

I didn't have the strength to curse a the W, and I couldn't think of a solution anymore. My heart, which had prepared for every possible scenario, knew it was over.

"Mrs. Mason," the voice said. "I'd like you to go back to the shower, get dressed. I'll instruct you on how to leave the building. It's been a pleasure."

48

Two days later, I was in my apartment staring at one of my old paintings, which I'd shredded to pieces. I needed to give way to my anger, and I'd worked hard on these paintings, so they helped me with conscious self-sabotage.

I wasn't the type to hurt myself or do something crazy. I was just a mother in unbearable pain, trying to find a way to accept the unacceptable. And I had to let my rage and disappointment out on something besides myself.

Since leaving the W, I stopped having a phone. It helped me isolate myself from the world. I'd turned it off and left it somewhere in the apartment.

Emma passed by this morning and told me how Katherine dropped the charges and that Tom Holmes charged someone else with the events of the African man's death. She told me about a convoluted story they cooked up, the kind you see in the news every day and roll your eyes. I couldn't care less.

Though she was glad to be alive, I couldn't pay attention to Emma's talk, so I asked her to leave. I didn't want to pretend to care or entertain anyone. I wanted to wallow in my misery.

Sitting crossed legged with my photographs of my father's eight pictures of me, I wished I knew how to get on the Runaway Train.

I'd even chatted with Lupita this afternoon online to find an answer, and she said she didn't know how to do it. She reminded me that Deji's disappointment with the W not accepting him was him trying to get on the Runaway Train. She also said that getting on it was expensive because faking a new life was a tedious and prolonged process.

The W only made an exception to those who were in dire need of it. I guess Deji convinced them finally, considering his situation.

"I mean a million pounds expensive," she said. "How Deji got this money, I have no idea."

"But didn't Andrew contact you," I said. "Then you must know how to contact him again."

"He contacted me through a stranger. A woman I met in the park told me what he needed to tell me. After that, I never saw her again. Besides, after you contacted the Igbo, they must have their eyes on you. Meaning, you contacting your son can get him killed."

Since then, I'd hung up, given up, and sat on the floor with Kyle Mason's photographs.

I stopped crying.

I stopped thinking.

What was the point?

I seriously considered Katherine for therapy. That's how desperate I had become. I needed someone to hypnotize me into acceptance. Into obedience. I needed to find a way to become one of the crowd, watch Netflix, eat snacks, trust the news, and be blind to the real workings of the world.

Being me wasn't working for *me* anymore.

Even Kyle Mason's photographs didn't bring me solace anymore. I was spoiled by a father who painted me into a beautiful image in his mind, over and over again. Maybe parents should stop loving their children so much. What was the point in giving them the world when the world would eventually take it away from them?

I flipped image after image, remembering Deji renumbering

them because of that one image he thought was better than the other. Which was it again?

"10, 9, 6, 7, 8, 5, 4, 3, 2, 1," he used to say.

Beautiful memories of my father talking about the one image that was the jackpot and how he sold more similar paintings to his clients by convincing them that 'one' was the original. In reality, only one of them was the *one*.

It had always been this incident that made me think Deji and my father could've formed a peculiar bond had my father not died. I imagined Deji and Andrew playing with the Runaway Train in that same spot next to me and Kyle Mason playing along in the living room.

It was the image of a perfect memory that never happened. Three generations of the perfect men in my life, right in front of my eyes—

Suddenly, an epiphany hit me. I called it an epiphany because it wasn't entirely logical.

I tilted my head to the couch in the living room where Jason once sat and begged me to look at Adaolisa's messages.

Wait!

I quickly rummaged through the photographs of my father's painting and picked up the image Deji thought was better than the other. He thought the eighth was better than the sixth.

I found it, staring at it as if it were the holy grail.

I raised it to the light and saw Deji's handwriting. He'd run an arrow into the number eight and had renumbered it six. Next to it read in faint and small letters, *"pm, Mo, Tu, We."*

8 pm, Mondays, Tuesdays, Wednesdays.

I jumped to my feet and went to find my phone, picking up from under two weeks of unattended laundry.

I clicked it on and waited forever for it to turn on. The battery was only on 5%. But it was all I needed.

I chose wifi and searched google for the 8 pm trains on Monday, Tuesdays, and Wednesdays. I searched many lines from Dorchester and London. There were too many options, and none of them ever turned out to be the train Deji and Andrew got on.

I googled the words 8 pm, Monday, Tuesday, Wednesday, and added runaway train. Finally, I found a single article that matched all terms — the rest checked two or three, but not all five phrases.

When I clicked on it, I found a long article about a transport company having been fined £300,000 after a 'runaway train' came within 2,000ft of crashing into a packed tube train.

Of course, this runaway train phrase didn't mean what I knew about the real Runaway Train.

Were Deji and Dad on the same page, trying to tell me something? Did I miss the mark eight years ago? Was this the train I needed to get on?

I tapped my foot, watching the phone charge lessen to 3%. Emma's warning about 'them' watching my every move on the phone troubled me. I had no choice. I reckoned to find out the truth first and then worry about surveillance later.

My eyes scanned through the article, trying to find a connection. I had to see it before my phone gave up on me.

The sentence midway read, "Had the runaway train hit the tube; it would have killed over thirty-five employees at the prestigious Welcome Home company."

My legs buckled underneath me. I dropped to the floor, trying to catch my breath.

1% left in the charging.

Time: 6:34 pm.

Nothing was stopping me from dashing out and going to that 8 pm train, but I needed one last confirmation.

I began to believe that this message wasn't made to be read eight years ago. It was made to be read on my wedding day when Andrew sent the other one to me. Jason may have been right about re-checking all of them. I'd told him they were all the same but were they?

I scrolled through my phone—nineteen messages from Adaolisa on behalf of Andrew that day.

Cha cha cha cha, choo choo train,
Rolling down the choo choo lane,

I hear your whistle blowing loud (choo choo)

10, 9, 8, 7, 6,

5, 4, 3, 2, 1

Mum N Pa go!

The same message nineteen times, over and over again, except one. Just one. It read:

Cha cha cha cha, choo choo train,

Rolling down the choo choo lane,

I hear your whistle blowing loud (choo choo)

10, 9, 6, 7, 8,

5, 4, 3, 2, 1,

Mum N Pa go!

There it was. My mind only saw what it expected to see. I'd always wondered why nineteen messages, but Kyle Mason always told me, and just like Deji said, one *of them was the jackpot.*

49

It was 7:33 pm when I arrived at the train station.

To my disappointment, the 8 pm train was out of service. But, of course, it was a Sunday. What had I been thinking?

Almost no passengers walked around this area. So it puzzled me why this lane was blocked on the days the train was out of service. When I asked one of the crew workers, he told me that this train, in particular, had been in so many near-accidents for years, especially since the incident with the W's crew.

"What do you mean by near accidents?" I asked.

"It's bonkers," the old man said. "Always close enough to clash with another train or change lanes or malfunction as if it's cursed."

This got me curious. I did what I've been best at lately and shoved the man ten pounds in his back pocket. Touching a stranger wasn't the best idea, but what else made sense anymore?

"Could you please let me past the closed area?" I almost pleaded with my eyes.

"That's a twenty," he astonishingly said, staring at me from top to bottom. "Fifty pounds if you plan on smoking pot or doing something kinky."

"Twenty then," I said and shoved him another ten in his hands this time.

He crumbled the money in the palm of his hand and coughed in my face, "I don't know why everyone likes this runaway train so much."

I didn't know what to say. The article called it a runaway train as well, so it wasn't like I expected him to be in on it — that was if I was right about it in the first place.

"A twenty will only get you to do whatever you do halfway," he said. "I'd sit by the third bank and wait if I were you."

"What are you talking about?"

"Wait for me when I start humming my song," he cut me off. "That'd be the signal for you to sneak in."

I watched him pretend to be cleaning farther away and closer to the crowd. He began singing with a cigarette between his teeth while waving his broom.

Choo Choo train. Choo Choo train. 1,2,3,4, or whatever the bloody hell this song says.

I guessed that he didn't even know the lyrics to the main rhyme, but I finally felt at home. I must have been on the right track.

I walked next to the empty train and sat on the third bank. There was no one in sight anywhere. I could've been easily mugged or killed without anyone noticing soon enough.

I reminded myself that the man had told me to sit and wait. Unless he was crazy, I was expecting someone.

8:44pm.

I was getting impatient.

Wait.

A big man covering half of his face under an Irish tweed cap sat next to me. It was as if he came out of nowhere.

I watched him sit by the far end of the bank and say nothing. I waited for a while, looking at him but he intentionally pulled to hide his face from me.

"I'm Kate," I said.

"U-huh," he nodded, staring away.

"Do you know me?"

"U-huh."

"Your tone is familiar," I said, trying to decipher the voice behind this mysterious man.

"U-huh."

"Am I on the right track ? — No pun inteded."

This time he said nothing.

"I mean, is this where Andrew wanted me to be?"

"U-huh."

"Why is your voice so familiar?"

He shifted his body farther away from me.

"Okay. I won't ask," I said. "Will I ever see my son and husband again?"

"U-huh."

I couldn't help myself from uttering a small but joyous laugh. It's hard to accept good things to happen when you've only experienced bad things for so long.

"How?" I asked, elated at this new feeling of hope.

Now he didn't reply again.

"Okay. Okay. I guess I have to ask a question you can answer with your too-familiar nods."

"Yup."

"I know it's Sunday, and I probably missed the train or Andrew, I don't know. I want to know if I can meet Andrew now."

"Uh-huh," he nodded this time.

"Will Andrew meet me here?"

He shook his head no for the first time.

"Then how am I going to meet him? But, wait. Maybe I should take another train since I was told Runaway Trains are everywhere?"

"Yup."

"Great. How will I know which one if you don't speak words?"

He said nothing.

"Sorry," I waved my hands. "I have to find out myself. I get it." I paused while an idea hit me. "Wait. The puzzle."

"U-huh."

"10, 9, 6, 7, 8—"

"Yup."

"The numbers reference time," I clicked my fingers.

"Warm."

"It's almost 9 pm so I assume the 6,7, and 8 are out of the question. They're only trains I missed."

"Warmer."

"So maybe the 9 pm train?"

"Yes," he said this time.

Even though I still had more questions, my heart almost stopped.

"I know you."

"Yes," he said, sounding happy about it.

"Say yes again?"

"I can say a better word, Snowflake."

This time the tears in my eyes brought me happiness, the kind I've never thought I could experience. My heart was fluttering with joy, gratitude, and so much hope.

"Say it," I smiled, crying. "The name I used to call you."

"Picasso," he turned sideways and smiled at me.

"Dad!" I threw myself in his arms, not knowing what else to do. I mean, I wanted to enjoy this surreal moment for infinity.

"Just don't be loud about it," he embraced me with his big arms. "I'm sorry for all you've been through."

"You're not dead!" I said through tears as I buried my face in his chest.

"Not yet," he chuckled, running his hands through my hair.

"But I was told you were killed in jail."

"There is a Runaway Train in jail, too. Sometimes in planes. Where'd you think the passengers of the Malaysian airplane disappeared a few years ago?" he said. "I was never a spy, Snowflake. Please believe me."

"I do believe you."

"I wrote codes in paintings to pass messages from the W to immigrants and from immigrants to their loved ones. Katherine's elite patients didn't like that, so she got rid of me."

"It's okay, dad. You're here with me."

He gently grabbed me by the shoulders to look at me, his face serious now, "Not for long."

"Why?"

"Andrew and Deji are waiting for you. Sorry again for never telling you. Deji's brother being announced unworthy of the Igbo's death happened suddenly. Deji never thought his brother would become a terrorist. Moreover, he never thought they'd come for Andrew."

"I don't want to know more," I said. "I get it. I will never understand the world I live in. I don't want to. I want to be with my son and husband."

"Good," he looked at his watch. "You have five minutes. Gate 10, the 9 pm train to Oxford."

"So soon? You won't come?"

"I have people to serve. Messages to pass along. Maybe someday," he said, then handed me a ticket in case I was going to object and force his hand to come with me. "A few minutes after you get on the train, a heist will occur. Don't resist it. They will take you hostage, and from there, they will take you to your family."

I recited his words to make sure I didn't forget the plan, then I had to ask, "Who paid for me getting on the train, Picasso?"

"Mila," he said.

"With Katherine's money? The trust fund?"

"A million pounds," he said. "That was her and Jason's plan from the beginning. She'd sacrifices four years of her life and take the money then get on the train to find her mother. But she reckoned you lost eight years of your life, away from your son already. She is a fighter. She still has time to get on the train."

"I'll make sure to find her mother when I find Deji. I promise I will help her get on the train. I swear."

"I know."

I nodded, wholeheartedly vowing to help her, "I'll miss you, Picasso."

"I'm always with you in my paintings," he said. "Even though I suck as a painter. Don't tell anyone, Snowflake," he gave me one last loving smile and disappeared back into the darkness.

50

I sat in the seat by the window on the train, the one Picasso, aka Kyle Mason, booked for me. The train took off, and the seat next to me remained free.

There weren't many people on the night train anyway. I had my eyes fixed, wondering which stop the heist would occur. My father didn't tell me.

My heartbeat fluctuated between anxiety and anticipation — and also fear that I still wasn't going to find my son and run into another lie, or worse, Tom Holmes or the Igbo showing up again.

I laced my hands together in an attempt to keep calm and waited.

Two stations later, a man in an expensive suit with a suitcase came on board. He sat a few rows before me. I reckoned he was a banker, not sure if he was also with the W or not.

I didn't care. I was here for my husband and son.

The train took off again, and it occurred to me that I hadn't asked my father where the thieves, or whatever they were called, were going to take me. I guess I was about to know soon.

Mila came to mind. I'd promised her to come back for her. And though I didn't know how, I wouldn't give up on her. Once I found my family — if I did — I swore I would find her mother and come back for her.

It still puzzled me why Natalie left Mila behind and why she never contacted her as Andrew did with me. I mean, I knew some of the story but not the whole. Then again, I reminded myself that I wasn't going to have all the answers in this life.

People usually were pissed off when they don't get the answers. However, if I'd learned anything in this journey, I'd say I wanted to do good in life, care for those I love, and let the world be. Unfortunately, I wasn't a hero. I didn't have the tools to help or save everyone. I wish I were more robust, more resourceful, but maybe I can be if I meet my family.

And as for Jason, I understood his motives. He didn't lie to me because he was a bad man. He was one in pain. The pain made him compromise his decisions. He wanted to find Natalie and help Mila. Did he really feel something for me, or was he faking it — or did he fool himself into feeling for me to overcome his agony?

In my heart, I will always remember him as a friend of pain. He did his best and sacrificed himself for the greater good.

I waited for the thieves at the next stop, but no one showed up. A few people came on board, including a young African man whose ticket was right next to me.

He asked to sit, looking worried and shy, and I nodded that he could.

He had black hair tied into a long braid. He was taller than me— way taller at his young age. I looked at him if he was one of the thieves or contacts, but he seemed oblivious to anything. He had brown eyes and read Catcher in the Rye, which wasn't a book someone his age read, but who was I to judge. I barely knew how the world around me worked.

"It's the next stop," he suddenly said, looking ahead like everyone else, as if we were spies in a movie.

"What happens at the next stop?" I asked. I wanted to test him in case the Igbo sent him. I mean, he looked like he could've been one of them.

"The man in the tailored suit and the brown suitcase," he said while checking his phone. "That's him."

"I knew there was something about him," I said, still hoping he wasn't with the Igbo and just pulling my leg.

I began to worry that sitting by the window had my corners. I couldn't escape if he were.

"Don't resist," he said, inexpertly holding my hand. "I'm here to help. They will take me with you."

As the train stopped, I hadn't had enough time to process, and I saw the masked African men enter with their guns.

The boy sensed my anxiety and squeezed my hands harder for assurance. No matter how I had been told what would happen, the heist scene scared the shit out of me. It was too believable that I ducked when they threatened everyone with their guns.

The boy ducked with me and looked at me in that awkward position. He seemed concerned, almost scared, and it made me feel as if I had done something wrong.

"We shouldn't be ducking like that, so it looks convincing enough to pick us up haphazardly."

"When will we meet my son after they pick us up?" I whispered, straightening back to my usual position.

The man in the mask pointed his gun at the boy and me, prompting us to come with him.

The boy squeezed my hand and sincerely smiled at me, "You've met him already, mum. Welcome, Home."

AFTERWORD

Thank you for reading the Runaway Train. As explained in the beginning, Deji's type of family exists. My friend told me about her own family back home, and I spent a year researching it. My friend and I are of African descent, so I genuinely don't mean to criticize or point fingers.

Facts:

The ongoing killing of African feudal families has never stopped until today. However, I can't say more. If this conflict has crossed over to other continents, I do not know of that.

I've interviewed several tribe members from the area to receive their firsthand experience. I found them to be either submissive to the situation or supporting it with pride. Most were submissive, feeling as if there was nothing they could do about it.

The shroud ceremony mentioned is authentic. It is usually done in an open space and is considered a huge event. Despite the ceremony being a real event, the fact that the ceremony within the book took place in the W is indeed fictional.

The last fact that I find most heart-wrenching is that there was no remorse in regard to the feudal killings. It was considered justice or God's will, or a fact of life that should be accepted and abided by.

There is no secrecy about it, for it is just a way of life. Only Western media doesn't bother mentioning it.

I like to write about resilient women, mothers, and daughters who overcome life's obstacles which is another inspiration for this story. When I was writing about Kate and developing her character, I purposely wrote her to have a unique way to navigate the madness that unfolded around her. I felt the need to downplay her a bit, not making her as strong or badass so as not to distract from the overall quest and secrecy within the tale. There is also the fact that things *happen to her*, especially in the first half of the book where she isn't instrumental in figuring things out. Again, I didn't see how an ordinary citizen could handle the situation differently. Her courage is revealed in her offering herself to die so she could save her son.

However, as her character developed and as the story unfolded, Kate did find her solace after all.

ALSO BY EMBER BLAKE

The Last Girl by Ember Blake

(previously published under the pen name: Nick Twist):

a gripping and emotional thriller that is based on true events. I wrote this thriller three years ago under the pen name Nick Twist if you want to check it out.

ABOUT THE AUTHOR

My pen name is Ember Blake and I appreciate you reading this book. Please review it, if possible, whatever you thought of the story. Your review helps the story and allows me to know what I'm doing right and what I need to work on in the future.

I try to keep my life private and be only present as an author who loves the craft and wants to keep learning and keep writing. If you enjoyed the book and want to know about upcoming stories or previous ones, please find me on Facebook or send me an email. Thank you again, dear reader, for your support.

You can still contact me on my Facebook Page:
https://www.facebook.com/emberblakefanpage
Or subscribe to my newsletter for my next book:
www.emberblake.com
Also don't hesitate to email me:
emblake88@hotmail.com
Thank you

MOVIE OPTION

During the writing, I've been approached a few times with offers to option Runaway Train for a movie. I appreciate that immensely, though I'm reluctant to accept the offer, as I've expressed before. (Reason being it does touch on certain minorities, and I don't want to be misunderstood. We live in relatively polarizing times, and I wish not to be part of more drama or pain to anyone.)

In any case, this section is for if you're still interested in offering the movie option. Maybe we can figure it out under certain circumstances and agreements of how the story would be filmed, in all fairness to all sides.

Please email me here: emblake88@hotmail.com with the subject title, 'Movie Option.' This is my personal email, not my agents or publisher.

sincerely,
Ember Blake

Printed in Great Britain
by Amazon